COMES THE DRAGON

Comes the Dragon

Published by Little Dozen Press
Stevensville, Ontario, Canada
www.littledozen.com

ISBN: 978-1-927658-40-6

COMES THE DRAGON

BOOK 2 OF THE PROPHET TRILOGY

by Rachel Starr Thomson

Little Dozen Press
2015

PROLOGUE

Sabrus Caelius looked down on his amassing army with a crooked gaze. A scar cut down the left side of his face, splitting his lip and pulling it up, cocking his expression. On another the effect might have been comical, but there was nothing comical about the general of the world's greatest military force.

He stood on the brow of the hill Quirinius, looking down on the broad plain between the hill and the sea, green shading into hazy blue beyond the dust of the legions massed before him.

Cohorts in their multiple hundreds stood in ranks; companies in their eighties; banners flying. Archers and spearmen, and beyond them, cavalry. The rectangular shields of the infantry, made of wood covered with taut skins and embossed with bronze, were nearly the height of the men themselves. When they stood side by side and locked shields, they were an impenetrable moving wall. When the sun flared upon their ranks, the bronze embossings blazed like fire.

There had never been an army like them, Sabrus thought. Not one of the great empires of old had boasted such a force. The companies spread out on every side, ten thousand men all told, and these were only two of his great legions. All in all he commanded a hundred thousand men—with their force magnified by their terrifying order, unity, and discipline.

No other man could have held their loyalty. There were too many; they were too diverse. They owed allegiance to others, other lands, other kindreds.

But Sabrus had promised them the world, and he would give it them.

He needed only to declare himself ruler of the Westland and the empire that was just within its grasp.

For a hundred years now the Westland had cultivated ties with other nations, forming trade alliances all along the coast of the sea and inland to the north and west. Alongside the trade, mercenary bands formed for protection and transport, coming under the leadership of the Westland's military—for a price, of course.

Quietly, slowly, the Westland grew richer and more powerful than any of its allies—and alongside them, the mercenary army grew. In number, force, and loyalty.

Sabrus, born with a sword in his hand, commanded their forces and one day recognized that he was staring empire in the face. All he had to do was centralize the army's loyalty and then assert power over all the nations they now protected—after becoming king, of course.

The current king of the Westland, Aulus Marius, had no ambition, few years, little vision. No one who loved him.

So he would not be hard to oust from his throne.

The senate would be harder to win to his side. But in the end, what could a gathering of mewling old men do against swords and spears and the force of an army that shone like the sun? What could they do against a vast mercenary army with all the riches of the world gleaming in their eyes?

     RACHEL STARR THOMSON

With the cohorts assembled and in place, every helmeted eye trained on the hill, Sabrus raised his arm in salute. Ten thousand men thundered in reply.

He would soon seize the throne, and the west would belong to him. Then all that remained was to turn his eyes eastward, across the sea to the desert lands and kingdoms on the other side. He had no doubt of the outcome. Their thrones, their peoples, and their gods would fall before him.

The tribesman would die before another night passed. Of that Alack felt certain.

He closed his eyes in misery, listening to the man's groans and occasional yells. The women and children gathered around the wounded man remained eerily silent, watching him die—or peering up at Kol Abaddon, edging closer to him, watching the prophet until he scowled at them and sent them scuttling back to the wounded warrior's side.

Every bone and muscle in Alack's body ached. If riding on a ship's deck had been unpleasant, it was far worse riding belowdecks with his hands bound and his back against the curving wooden hull, sticky with pitch, that rose and fell and threw him with the waves, crammed in amongst the other captives for days and nights without number, listening to a man die by degrees—

Worse, he thought, than anything he could have imagined when he apprenticed himself to Kol Abbadon.

The slavers descended into the murky light of the hold twice a day to feed them gruel and water. With their hands bound and the ship tossing, the gruel slopped, and the mess added to the misery.

The former merchant captain, now bundled in beside Alack and Kol Abaddon like one more sack of meal, spent most of his time with his eyes closed and his head resting against the hull. He did not even twitch a muscle when the dying man went into a raving fit.

The captain seemed impervious to the tossing of the ship; perhaps ability to move with the water was bred into him. It was not at all bred into the shepherd boy from the Sacred Land, the prophet-in-training who had never felt so far from home.

Kol Abaddon had not said two words since their capture. Alack itched with questions and fears, but the prophet was surlier than ever. He glared at the tribespeople who seemed to expect something from him and ignored Alack entirely.

Though day and night were alike beneath the ship's deck, Alack estimated by the frequency of feedings that they had been three days at sea since the slavers took them captive in the tribal village. His heart ached for the women and children and the few men in the hold with them. He could not speak their language, but he understood their voices and their eyes as they whispered to each other, as they glanced at him and at the prophet. It seemed especially cruel that they should be attacked and enslaved after Kol Abaddon had restored them all to each other such a short time ago. He reminded himself that these same tribesmen had attacked and meant to kill them, and their lives had been saved only by Kol Abaddon's intervention—but their wives? Their little ones?

Slavery was not always the worst of lives—great poverty with freedom was generally worse. And yet . . .

He glanced at the prophet. Kol Abaddon rested his shaggy head against the hull in the murky shadows; he seemed to be asleep. Or else he was just ignoring the tribespeople.

The prophet had worked miracles on the island. Could he truly do nothing now?

     RACHEL STARR THOMSON

Alack's bruised head ached, and he did his best to dismiss his thoughts and concentrate on stilling his stomach and protecting his sea-battered body from being battered yet again.

The dying man let out a long, protracted groan that made Alack's skin crawl.

"We'll be nearly there," the captain said.

Alack squirmed to a straighter posture. "What did you say?"

The captain's accent was thick, and he spoke in the merchant pidgin familiar to all the nations that ringed the Great Sea. "We've been three and a half days at sea. If they are headed for the slave market in Avia, we'll be in port by sundown tonight."

Alack's stomach tightened at the news. "And then what will happen to us?" he asked.

"We'll be sold into slavery. Unless you have friends to help you."

"Not in Avia, no," Alack said. He eyed Kol Abaddon and was about to add, "Unless he knows someone," but he shut his mouth. If the prophet knew anyone in the Westland, he hadn't said so. As far as Alack knew, Kol Abaddon still intended to speak to the king—present circumstances notwithstanding.

The captain closed his eyes again. "The gods have been against us all this voyage," he said.

"Our God has not," Alack said. "He blinded the eyes of the attackers."

"True. But he's gone absent now, hasn't he?" the captain said. "That's the gods for you. Fickle."

Alack leaned his head on his knees, ignoring the ache in the small of his back and his tailbone from sitting in this posture for so long, and told himself the captain was wrong and the Great God was not absent.

He was merely inactive for the moment—inactive and silent.

Much like his prophet, Kol Abaddon.

Keeping his voice too low for anyone else to hear, Alack finally dared address his mentor.

"What are we going to do?" he asked.

To his surprise, Kol Abaddon didn't ignore the question. "We are going to give the king a message," he said.

"We are on our way to a slave market," Alack pointed out.

"Just a stepping stone."

Lowering his voice even further, Alack said, "But how do you know? Why is this the Great God's plan? Why not just let us go with the captain all the way?"

"He meant to double-cross us," Kol Abaddon said, his voice barely discernible. "He would have held us for ransom or sold us and done us greater harm than these men will do."

Alack blinked. "What? How do you know that?"

"The Great God showed me."

"When?"

"Before we boarded his ship."

"Then why did we board it?" Alack said, now fighting to keep his voice down.

Kol Abaddon's lips twitched. "It was going to the Westland."

His mentor was laughing at him, and somehow that made Alack feel better.

He peered down the row at the captain, who still looked like he was sleeping but was most likely not. Would the man really have double-crossed them?

     Rachel Starr Thomson

Yes, he thought, he would have.

The wounded tribesman's groaning rose in pitch and intensity, and the women sitting around him joined in, their voices a high, unnerving wail.

The captain sat up suddenly and pounded the side of the ship with his bound hands. "Would you all shut up!" he yelled. "Shut up before I find a way to beat you all senseless!"

His threats only sent a group of the children crying, and then the entire hold was filled with wailing, crying, screaming, and under it all, the dying man's groans. Alack's nerves had never known such a sound. Nor had his heart ever heard such despair.

But then—the eyes glancing their way again. With expectation. With hope.

He scooted closer to Kol Abaddon and said in a low voice, "We should help them."

Kol Abaddon did not even open his eyes. "Hush," he said. "You speak trouble. You want the captain to hear you? He'll be ransomed in Avia; he can still make trouble for us. We have a mission."

"But these people—"

"We owe them nothing."

Alack scooted back to his original spot, thought for a moment longer, and then, unable to stand the sound of the tribespeople's despair, lurched back to Kol Abaddon's side. "You are the Great God's prophet!" he said. "You blinded eyes for their sake. Helped them. Why can't you do it again?"

At the prophet's silence, Alack followed the captain's example and thumped his hands against the hull. Ignoring the self-inflicted pain, he said angrily, "You're the one who told me I might be a savior, not just a prophet."

"Then you help them," Kol Abaddon said. "But keep us out of trouble in doing it." He opened his eyes and trained them—intense and dark—on his apprentice. "It's not magic, the power of the Great God. We owe these people nothing. And yes, you may have some . . . special role. In the Sacred Land. That doesn't make you a god. Or me."

Alack shut his eyes and leaned against the hull, breathing hard through his nose to calm his anger—an emotion which, he was beginning to realize, was at least nine parts panic. He begged the Great God to do something, or at least to quiet the wailing.

Moments later, two slave traders descended from above and dealt out threats, blows, and orders for silence. The wailing stilled.

Alack closed his eyes and rested his head on his knees, banging bone against bone as the ship pitched in the waves once again. The murk of the hold returned to a miserable quiet, broken only by one man's uncontrollable groans.

⸻ ◆ ⸻

True to the captain's estimation, the ship docked in Avia that same evening as the sun was setting in the west, its rays spilling over the land onto the eastern sea.

"Up! Out! Single file, all of you!" the slavers shouted. Alack stood awkwardly. The movement of forty-some captives trying to stand at once created a shuffling, overcrowded tangle of bumping and nudging and throwing one another off-balance. Every muscle and bone protested as Alack stretched his legs for the first time in three days.

Following the ship's captain and Kol Abaddon, and leading the way for the women and children who did not seem to know quite how to stand in a line, he shuffled above deck. The light hurt his eyes and lifted his heart all at once.

 RACHEL STARR THOMSON

The last he saw of the hold was several of the stronger women trying to lift the dying man with their hands tied.

They had docked in the midst of a bustling port, and the city lined the banks of the inlet on every side, plastered brick buildings clustered as far and deep as Alack could see. People were everywhere, shouting, carrying, fighting, laughing. Cattle and donkeys weaved in and out of the crowds, some led by their owners or slaves, some wandering free. He expected camels but saw none; this was not his desert home.

This was Avia, capital city of the Westland. The shepherd boy had crossed the sea.

The port smelled of the flesh of man and beast, mingled with the stronger scents of salt and spices and fish and the acrid waste of too many people in one place. On a street corner not far from the docks, four boys played reedy flutes and clashed cymbals wildly, and bystanders danced. Soldiers stood in threatening clusters everywhere Alack looked. Was there an entire army in this city?

Moments after Alack's feet touched the dock, the slavers called a halt. He stood in the light of the setting sun with a frightened line of women and children behind him, all of them chattering and calling to one another in low voices. The slavers conversed with men by the shipside for a long time.

When Alack had begun to fidget with impatience, he heard a voice hailing them. He turned his head and saw two men in merchant's robes approaching, hands raised in greeting.

The old ship's captain shouted a hail back. In minutes the slavers cut his bonds, a bag of money changed hands, and the captain was released to his friends. He spoke with them in low voices for a moment, and all three turned, trained their eyes on Alack and Kol Abaddon, and stared hard.

A second later, they were gone—vanished into the crowds and the quickly fading light. Shadows stretched over the city and the harbor, where torches were just beginning to flicker to light, and Alack strained his eyes in vain to see where the captain had gone.

One of the slavers shoved Kol Abaddon forward. "Keep moving."

He did, leading a bewildered line of slaves the rest of the way down the gangplank to the dock and from there to the shore. When Alack's feet touched solid ground, it heaved under him and nearly threw him off balance. He yelped with surprise and indignation—after all this time, that land should feel like sea was a nasty trick.

To his surprise, Kol Abaddon turned his head. "Don't be afraid," he said.

The lights of oil lamps and braziers were coming on all over the city as the sun sank, lighting up the banks and the gentle hills beyond them. The noise of Avia only intensified as the slavers pushed their line of captives into the thick of the crowds, along the shoreline and then up the narrow streets into the city. Headed for the slave market, Alack supposed.

Slavery was not foreign to him. His people, the Holy People, practiced it just like everyone else in the world, even though they had a self-righteous tendency to turn their noses up at mention of the trade—like if they didn't *talk* about it, it wouldn't matter that they practiced it.

Alack's father, Naam, had told him that long ago, the People refused to enslave one another—they had owned servants of other races only, and even then, had considered it better that all men should be free. On top of that, the Great God had given laws of release that limited any slave's term of service. But even the People rarely practiced those distinctions anymore, and Alack had little hope that the Westlanders would hold to any similar ideals.

Inspired by Kol Abaddon's example, he turned his head and said, "Don't be afraid" to the woman behind him. Likely she couldn't under-

     RACHEL STARR THOMSON

stand his words, but she seemed to take comfort from his tone, and he heard murmurs from the others behind him. He turned his head forward again as he walked, satisfied.

The crowds in the city were so thick and so boisterous that they threatened to cut the captives off from one another. The slavers kept up a constant stream of shouts and violence, cuffing and clubbing slaves, cattle, and passersby alike anytime the line threatened to break. Alack entertained a brief hope of getting away in the confusion, but the slavers knew their business and managed to keep their captives together and moving forward. He stumbled over something in the street, and a blow to his shoulder kept him going before he'd even had time to figure out what was tripping him. At least the ground was starting to settle down—it had been pitching under him every minute since he stepped off the boat.

The journey took them up a meandering path through close-built, three-story apartment buildings, all of them with people peering out, waving hands, dropping things. Water stains ran down the sides of every building from waste tossed out the open windows. Smoke from braziers filled the air, and Alack fought to keep his senses attuned as his head swam.

Their drivers turned them up another side street, this one climbing a steep slope, and then the captives nearly fell, one by one, into a square pit dug out before them. Alack climbed down gingerly, as carefully as he could with his hands bound. There was barely enough room for them all, and they packed in shoulder to shoulder and back to back. He watched his feet, afraid of trampling one of the smaller children.

The dying man was lowered down by three of the women and one of the two other tribesmen who had been taken alive. Then a heavy iron grate was pulled over the pit, the rings of a chain fastened it to the ground, and guards took their places where their shadows fell over the pit in the confused light of torches.

They had arrived.

The newcomers shuffled and turned, trying to make more room. They managed to open a few inches here and there, and Alack let out a breath he hadn't known he was holding. If stars shone overhead, they could not be seen from here. They were crowded out by the tall buildings, the smoke, the city lights.

Kol Abaddon's hand came down on Alack's shoulder, clamped hard, and dragged him several feet through the tightly packed group into a corner. It seemed miraculous that he had even found a way through the press. But somehow he had, and in the corner it was a little easier to breathe, a little more private, with earthen walls behind Alack's back and to one side of him. He gazed out at the shuffling, moaning mass of shadows, and he heard himself groan.

Kol Abaddon grunted and said, "Do you feel for yourself or for them?"

"For them," Alack said.

"Why not for yourself?"

He turned and looked at his mentor, struggling to make out his familiar features in the shadows. "Because I am not afraid. We have a mission from the Great God. Like you, I know we will fulfill it."

Kol Abaddon nodded with a grunt. "Good."

"What will happen to them?" Alack asked.

"I don't know."

And you don't care, Alack thought. He wasn't even sure Kol Abaddon cared about their own people and the terrible threat of judgment they were under. But then—did Alack? If he really cared, why was he here? Miles and miles from home in a land he had never imagined seeing, preparing to give a message from the Great God to a foreign king he cared nothing about?

          RACHEL STARR THOMSON

He leaned against the wall, grateful that it did not buck and pitch like the ship. After the voyage and now this, even being sold might feel like a relief.

He held onto that thought until he recognized some of the moving shadows as children and heard an infant crying. For many, or most, of these families, being sold would mean losing everyone they loved.

His heart sank, and tears pricked at his eyes. He didn't bother fighting them away. Though these people were strangers, and not one of them from his own race or his own city, down here in this pit they were all equals, all facing a future that was unsure, all facing the reshaping of who they were by forces not of their own choosing. With all his heart he wished he could take them all with him.

As though he could read his thoughts, Kol Abaddon said quietly, "You cannot save the world. You can only be faithful to the Great God's call, and watch him do what he will do through you, in whatever way he chooses to do it."

The darkness above deepened to full night, and still no stars. The dying man had ceased groaning; he breathed now in a terrible, guttural rasp. Those who sat around him—his family?—said nothing, did nothing.

Alack had wanted nothing for days so badly as to stretch his legs, but now his muscles ached, and he slid back down to the ground. It was damp, the earthen walls were damp, and he shivered. With the sea so close, the very air was wet. His body ached for the desert, and his heart did the same. For the desert and for freedom.

Alack slept, and he dreamed.

He saw the captives in the pit, crammed in next to each other, and each shone with varying light. Some were dim, like a lamp flame about to snuff out, others brighter, one or two brilliant. Something like a tendril of smoke or mist moved in their midst; he thought perhaps they were breathing it out—or in. It might be the fuel for the lights in them, or else the smoke of the same. He could not tell. He felt a sense of presence—a holiness, a nearness. They breathed something that was not mere air, something that *lived* around them.

His eyes shot open at the sound of the warrior in his death throes.

As though someone had opened a spigot, the horrible wailing of grief and despair began again.

And this time, the tribespeople begged.

As many as could reach him threw themselves at the prophet's feet, begging in words Alack could not understand. Alack himself was forgotten, ignored. Kol Abaddon motioned with his hands for them to stop, to leave him be. His eyes flashed with anger. The slaves began to beat their chests; some pounded their heads against the side of the pit and the floor.

The warrior gave out one last gargled cry and died.

They all heard the sound of his breath leaving his body—sucked into a terrible, dark vacuum.

And then the mood in the pit shifted, from pleading to anger, from hope to threat.

Alack saw it clearly even in the deep shadows. Kol Abaddon had betrayed their last hope.

He moved himself in front of the prophet, suddenly afraid. These were only women and children, but he knew them to be a violent people.

And yet he was angry with Kol Abaddon too.

When no immediate threat came against them—though the air filled with bitter murmurs amid the sobs and cries—he turned on the prophet and opened his mouth to accuse him.

Of letting a man die when he could have stopped it.

 RACHEL STARR THOMSON

Of not even trying to help.

Kol Abaddon heard the accusation without words. "There is no power for it," he snapped. "It isn't magic, I tell you; I cannot call up the power of the Great God at will."

"Maybe because you don't want to," Alack said, his eyes filling with tears. He tried to shove his way to the dead man, to pay his respects somehow. To redeem himself, his mentor, and even his people in the eyes of these captives who had looked to him for hope. He heard himself calling into their grief, talking to it—"Don't fear! Don't be afraid!"

Even as he stumbled through the cramped crowd toward the dead man, his vision shifted, and he saw not women and children, but sheep. Sheep, wooly and weary with dust and sand; sheep, limping and exhausted from the journey; sheep, their dark eyes desperate with thirst.

Sheep; and he, Alack, was a shepherd; and he wanted nothing more than to help them.

They moved for him. He knelt beside the dead man. In the faint light from torches above, he could make out the ugly, swollen wound that had killed him, a deep gash across his chest and shoulders. His tears fell. His helplessness, his total inability to make even the tiniest difference for the man, choked him.

"And what would you do if you could get them out of this pit?" Kol Abaddon called from the corner. "What would you do if you could save them? Would you become a chieftain? How would you feed them? Clothe them? Do you imagine you would pilot another ship to take them all home—where they no longer have husbands or fathers to care for them? Think your desires through, boy!"

Alack ignored him. Surrounded by the mourning tribe, he huddled down and prayed that the Great God would help him help these people.

CHAPTER 2

Nadab the Trader was angry, and equally, he was afraid. His anger had two objects: his daughter, and whoever had stolen her away. Of the identity of the latter he was unsure: it might be Alack, the shepherd boy who loved Rechab, or it might be Flora Laurentii Infortunatia, the brazen merchantwoman who had practically swindled Rechab's services away from him.

His fear had only one object: the god Kimash and his malevolent enforcers.

If Nadab thought too deeply, he might find that he was also angry at himself. He had, after all, sold Rechab for a wife to the high priest of Kimash of his own volition, attracted by the money and the prestige and the promises of power in such an alliance. He was one of the Holy People and knew that such an alliance went against everything in his history and in his veins, and yet, had he not traded blood for money long ago?

He chose not to think that deeply—to keep his emotions fixed on easier targets as he searched for some sign of his daughter in the wilderness that was so much of the Sacred Land.

He wore mourning garb for his slain household for three days, then discarded it. Better to keep his eyes on today, and the future, rather than weeping over yesterday. In the present and future were his own chances of staying alive and somehow redeeming the disaster of Rechab's betrothal.

In the past were only ashes, no good to him now.

With the one servant left to him alive, he had packed himself up and quickly taken the road into the wilderness. The move was as much symbolic as practical: he wanted to demonstrate to Kimash that he would not waste a moment obeying his orders. Equally, he wanted to put distance between himself and Kimash's enforcers—though he feared they would be tracking him even now, with terrifying stealth. Those two objects reached, he was forced to come to terms with the fact that he had no sure idea where Rechab had gone or even where to begin looking for her.

He sat now on the brow of a hill, looking down on a small town near the base of a small, desolate mountain. He had sent his servant ahead of him to speak to the village elders and learn whether Rechab had passed through. In the weeks since he had been searching, they had stopped in many such villages already, all to no avail. That was hardly a surprise. If she had run off with Alack, they would have taken pains to stay hidden, and the shepherd boy knew the wilderness far too well to be easily rousted. If she *had* gone with Flora Laurentii she would be far easier to discover, but no one would know that for certain—if she had gone with Flora, it had been secretly. So he might track the governor's sister to the far eastern edge of the Sacred Land only to discover that Rechab was not with her.

He was only one man, he thought as he watched the lights of the village winking to life in the dusk—small public fires in the center of the town, and oil lamps in some of the windows. One man, trying to track one wayward child across a land big and twisted enough to be lost in forever.

     RACHEL STARR THOMSON

And all with the threat of death hanging over his head and evil men eager to carry it out.

His stomach turned at the momentary thought that he was seeking out Rechab in order to turn her over to those same men. That his youngest daughter would live the rest of her life in their company and under their control—provided they let her live and did not kill her in anger for her flight.

He had always seen Rechab as an asset, one who would bring him greater wealth and power. She was a beauty, and he had invested in educating and refining her. He had never considered that in selling her, there would also be a price to pay.

Groaning a little, he turned his mule away from the view of the village. He did not want to think like this. Did not want to consider his actions, past or future. He simply wanted to find Rechab and do what he had to do.

If only the scouts Aurelius had sent out had returned before Kimash's enforcers came. He might have had an answer to give then, or even Rechab herself to hand over, instead of being forced on this fool's errand.

This time at least, when his servant returned from the town he had news.

"The old women know," Lethem said. "They have been whispering their rumors for some time. But there are two rumors—quite different."

"Tell me," Nadab said.

"They say Flora Laurentii passed by, and indeed there was a young woman in the train they had not seen before. They are sure your Rechab went with her."

Nadab nodded. The journey to find Flora would be long—but at least this gave him a clear goal. The desert community where Flora dwelt would not be hard to find, and it was not a terribly distant journey from here.

"And the other?"

"One of Aurelius's scouts passed through," Lethem said. "Closed-lipped and pale, they said. Would say nothing about his errand but cryptic remarks. But they filled him with wine and got his tongue loosed. He says he found your daughter far to the south—traveling alone with a man, and not a young man, but an old one. But he would not say what happened after he found them. He did not bring her back with him, that is certain."

Nadab's mind struggled to parse the conflicting reports. Enough time had passed that Rechab might have left Flora and traveled south again—but he could not imagine his fearful daughter roaming into the wilderness on her own. It would be one thing if the messenger had found her with Alack. But with an old man? What could that possibly mean?

"What do you make of it, Lethem?" Nadab asked.

The old servant sniffed. "I think the messenger was mistaken. The old women poked at him but could get few details out; they think he did not see the girl clearly. And he is hiding something. I think he is bringing a rumor back to Aurelius in hope of reward, but in truth he found nothing. If you will find Rechab, look for her to the east, with Flora Laurentii. It is the surest word you have."

Nadab nodded, his mind uneasy. Lethem was right—the scout's cryptic report was little to no help, at least in the form in which he was hearing it.

"Can we lay hold of Aurelius's messenger to hear for ourselves?" Nadab asked.

"He'll be in Bethabara by now." Lethem could not hide a shudder. "I would not return there, my lord, empty-handed."

 RACHEL STARR THOMSON

His advice was right. If nothing else, Flora Laurentii's far-off home offered just that advantage: it was far off. Far enough away from Bethabara that if the worst happened, Nadab might even be able to escape the Sacred Land and find a new start beyond its borders before Kimash tracked him down and exacted a more personal blood price for Rechab's flight.

━━━◆◆◆━━━

For the first week of her captivity in the camp of Amon the Southern Trader, Flora was kept in a richly woven but barren tent, with only a mat to sleep on and a single blanket to cover her. There had been cushions when she arrived, but they were removed, making it more clearly a prison cell. Guards stood watch all around the exterior. Far too many, she thought, for one woman. What did Amon expect her to do, fight her way out?

If she had a weapon, she just might have tried. But as it was, she had nothing but her wits, and even those were failing her, for she had no one to outthink, outspeak, or outfox. Joachim, her old and faithful servant, was being kept somewhere else in the camp. She worried for him but did not think Amon would go back on his word not to harm him. At least not without some purpose, and that, he would tell her about.

She did her best to ignore the two-headed figure of Kimash woven into the side of the tent, though it leered down at her all hours of the day. There were terrors in that figure, in those faces. She refused to give up holding them at bay.

Sometimes in the middle of the night, her whole spirit grew aware of the grotesque image above her. Flora had never been one to tremble in the presence of a threat, but in the tiny hours of the night, the fear conjured by the picture of the god of the Hills made the air oily and thick.

COMES THE DRAGON 27

The worst of it was that in the long, dragged-out hours, away from everything that had accoutered her life for many years—both the rich trappings of wealth and privilege that she wore when a merchant and the stark rituals of prayer, fasting, and solitude-amid-community that she kept when a pilgrim—she could not find refuge where she had always found it: in prayer to the Great God. The Great God had cast her out of Essea, and her only wrong had been in trying to protect the girl who now bore her name and commanded her retinue somewhere far away.

In the dark hopelessness of Amon's tent, Flora raged at that—at her exile. In the even deeper darkness that was the middle of the night when she could not sleep, she clenched her fists and steeled herself against greater anger, greater pain, for she felt that after all, it was unlikely the Great God even heard her rage. She was, in the end, nothing more than a bit of dust that had never wanted to accept its own insignificance.

But those dark hours wore off in the day, and then Flora simply paced and fretted and occasionally called curses on Amon's head and threatened his guards if they didn't get her an audience with their master before she went mad.

At length, she got it.

A servant dressed in purple appeared without warning in the door of her tent and bowed slightly. She cast a wrathful eye upon him from her mat, where she was sitting cross-legged, her woolen skirts demurely over her knees.

"Could you not be bothered to warn a woman before bursting in upon her unannounced?"

He ignored her. "The master wishes you to take the midday meal with him."

Flora thought of throwing Amon's request in his face, and just as quickly thought better of it. "Bring me a washbowl, then, and water. I'll not eat anything wearing a week's worth of dust."

 Rachel Starr Thomson

The servant bowed his head slightly and vanished as silently as he had come in. What seemed only an instant later, he returned bearing a golden washbasin, which he held out without a word.

"Talkative, aren't you?" Flora asked, taking the basin gingerly. Water splashed over the edge, but the servant seemed impervious. He held up three fingers and disappeared, the tent flap stirring behind him as though troubled by the slightest of breezes.

Flora washed—hurriedly—and was not surprised when the servant reappeared exactly three minutes later and said, "Come."

Amon's merchant caravan had not left the valley oasis where Flora had been brought upon capture. Ornamented tents created an organized temporary city. Camels stepped languorously amid the palm trees lining a spring and pool nearby, and armed guards, many on horseback, circled the encampment.

In the very center, Amon's tent was grand and imposing. She held her head a little higher as she entered behind the servant.

Amon was seated on cushions at a low table spread with dried fruit, roasted quail, fish, and nuts. Flora almost swooned at the sight. Amon had been feeding her—a nomad's diet of dried meat strips and a few dates. She hadn't realized how hungry she had actually grown in the shadows of her woven prison.

"Welcome," Amon said. His tone was unhurried, relaxed. He held up a hand when she made a move to sit down, stopping her, and picked up a bundle from the ground. Brilliant scarlet—silk, she thought.

"Before you join me," he said, raising the bundle toward her. "You may have the privacy of my chambers. Put this on."

"I washed," Flora said, resisting the urge to fold her arms like a sulking child. "Isn't that good enough for you?"

A muscle in his face twitched. "Your . . . homespun offends me."

"It's been good enough all this time. What has it been, Amon, a week?"

"I had matters to deal with. I apologize for neglecting you."

"Nonsense. You were trying to offend me."

He smiled. She was struck, not for the first time, by the way his smile stopped short of his eyes.

"A pity I have failed," he said dryly. "The time for neglect is over. I wish you to dress."

She turned up her nose at the rich scarlet. "I am humbling myself."

"And failing royally, for you are prouder than ever."

He stretched out the bundle once again. "You are not mistress here, Lady Infortunatia. I suggest you do as I say."

With a curt nod, she reached out for the bundle, making Amon rise a little to hand it to her. Silk indeed—smooth and soft. She closed her eyes for a split second, relishing it and then hating herself for doing so.

She dropped the bundle as though it were an asp. Amon raised a penciled eyebrow. "Is something wrong?"

"I am here as a prisoner, as you have so kindly reminded me, and you took me as such while I was on a pilgrimage. My pilgrimage is not ended, so I will remain clothed as a pilgrim."

"I am offended that you dress as you do," Amon said. "As are my servants. We all, in fact, are offended to see you playacting at something you are not."

Her eyes flashed green fire even as an inward knife, dug deep into her soul two weeks ago when she was cast out of Essea, wiggled a little deeper. "Now I am offended," she said.

He smiled again. "I am glad to see you have not lost your spirit. When we picked you up out of the desert, you seemed . . . cowed."

   RACHEL STARR THOMSON

"You were threatening my life, as I recall."

"I am surprised that would cow you."

It hadn't. Not really. She turned away a little so he couldn't see her eyes. The fear she had felt then was for others—Joachim, Rechab. For herself she felt only loss, rejection. When Rechab took her name, she'd thought for a moment that having lost her home could mean something new—something free, some new path the Great God would have her walk. When Amon snatched that freedom away, all her hope went with it. She was only refuse after all. Only an outcast. Only one too proud and too foreign to live in the presence of the Great God of the Sacred Land no matter how she tried to please him.

But Amon was baiting her now, and she didn't know how not to rise to it.

She cast a withering eye on the scarlet bundle on the floor. "I will do as you wish," she said, "but you must accommodate a request of mine also."

"Speak it," Amon said, sounding almost bored.

"I want a place to pray. Somewhere that Kimash does not glower down at me."

"I told you," Amon said, "Kimash is on the ascendant. You could not do better than to worship in his presence."

"Which is a thing I will never do, and you know that as surely as you know that you cannot change a leopard's spots."

"A place to pray," Amon repeated slowly.

"Give me a tent without any of your images woven into its sides, or a place outside with a guard. I care not. I pray three times a day, always, and three at night."

"I feel for the guard."

She bent down and picked up the scarlet bundle. "We are agreed, then."

At this Amon set down the wine goblet he had been holding in his right hand and laughed. He shook his shaven head in the soft light of the oil lamps. "Do you even know that you are a captive here? Flora Laurentii, I pity the *god* who hears from you six times a day."

He picked his goblet back up and waved in the direction of his chamber with his other hand. "Go, dress yourself. A meal awaits."

In the privacy of his chamber, sounds from without muffled by heavy curtains, Flora paused as she reached for the red dress. The fire in her belly died down in the close, stuffy stillness, and she fingered the material thoughtfully. It was so soft—so luxurious. The moment she put it on Flora the pilgrim would cease to be.

I am humbling myself, she had told Amon. But he was right—it hadn't worked.

No more than half a lifetime spent cloistered in the desert, praying and doing penance in an attempt to become truly holy, had worked.

Why had she insisted on a place to pray? He was right—the Great God had no interest in her continual coming.

And yet, she set her jaw as she shook out the dress and let its long folds unfurl before her. Lamplight brought out the deep richness of the red. The Great God might have no interest in her coming, but come she would until the day he struck her dead for it. The daughter of Florus Laurentinus had long ago made herself a worshiper of the Great God, and that was what she would be—the most stubborn worshipper, perhaps, that he had ever had.

When Flora reentered Amon's eating chamber, it was with the full knowledge that her beauty was stunning.

The dress was Westlandish—baring her arms and shoulders, falling

  RACHEL STARR THOMSON

in long folds to the floor. Her thick black hair curled in glossy waves down her back.

Amon looked up at her as she entered and waited as she approached. Just before she reached the low table, he wordlessly held up something more.

A golden bracelet.

She took it and slipped it on, then carefully knelt at the table.

He poured her a goblet of wine, seemingly pleased. "You look yourself again," he said.

"I am myself in the desert, where I dress in plain linen and wool. This is a costume," she answered.

"You are wrong," he told her, handing her the cup. She did not sip from it. "For a woman of great wisdom and power, Flora Infortunatia, you do not know yourself."

"And you do?"

Her face burned even as she asked the question. Their interaction was skewing too far in a direction she did not like—becoming flirtatious. She had to remember that the balance of power here was all on Amon's side, that she could not excuse herself and leave him waiting on her anytime she liked, nor could she call one of her armed guards to remove him from her presence.

Amon regarded her for an uncomfortably long time. She kept her gaze averted, refusing to play his game—whatever it was.

"You are here," he said at last, "under my power, until I can discern the best way to make use of you for purposes of extortion. That does not surprise you, I know. You have made extracting money from you surprisingly difficult; I will find a way eventually. But I have decided that rather than keeping you locked away, I would like for you to join me as my equal—though guarded, of course. You may have a place to pray; you may in fact have the run of the camp. If you attempt to run away, we will kill your servant, who does not have your freedom."

She nodded, her face burning again—just as much with anger as embarrassment this time. Amon knew her well enough to know that threatening Joachim would leash her more effectively than threatening her own safety.

"You will eat with me," he continued, "at noon and evening. I will leave you to breakfast on your own, as I am occupied in the mornings."

She nodded again.

"I will see to it that you have wash water, food, and clothing—clothing appropriate to who you are. Station, my lady, is a necessary and important thing. I would rather you did not dress like a slave in front of mine."

"I am not better than they are," Flora said.

He smiled indulgently. "You know as well as I do how fatuous a statement that is. You are a hundred times the superior of any of them—of all in this camp but me."

"Your slaves . . ." It had suddenly come back to Flora that if Amon was here, so were his servants.

Including the one who had attacked her in Essea.

Amon seemed to read her thoughts. "Yes, he lives, and he is here. I told you, did I not? He is possessed by a spirit of divination. He is useful to me."

Flora shook her head, at a loss for words for once. Her soul smarted at the thought of the slave, and not only because he had tried to kill her and bruised a few ribs in the process. Rather, his presence fingered her as a fraud.

"Something about him troubles you," Amon said. "I assure you he is no threat to you here—my men are watching him under penalty of

     RACHEL STARR THOMSON

their own lives."

"I thought—" she said. She stopped, decided she had nothing to lose, and said, "I thought I had delivered him. It pains me to know I was wrong."

"Delivered him?" Amon asked, his eyes showing enlightenment. "You mean drove the spirit out?"

"Yes," Flora said, finally taking a sip of her wine. She needed it.

Amon merely smiled. "You did," he said.

She almost spat the wine out. "What?"

"You ruined him—he was useless to me for weeks. Nearly the whole trek across the desert to Essea, following you and that girl, he was nothing but a mere man."

"Then how—what—"

"There is a principle in nature," Amon said. "Perhaps you have seen it. If you put an empty thing in water, the water fills it. If you dig a hole in sand, the sand rushes back in. Emptiness does not remain empty—always something will come back to fill it. My slave did not ask to be 'delivered.' We helped him be filled again."

"You helped—" she closed her eyes, suddenly sick to her stomach. "What did you do to him?"

"Nothing a follower of the Great God would have any pleasure in hearing about," Amon said. He picked up a date and turned it in his fingers. "He is good as new. Perhaps a bit more violent than before. But you, Flora—you should not underestimate yourself. You see, I spoke true—you are a woman of great power. You, a Hill Woman by nature, excel in the religion of the Holy People. And that intrigues me."

He set the date down, placed both palms on the table, and leaned forward, his eyes growing more intense. "I am a student of all things divine," he said. "You know that as well as any. But the Holy People have always disappointed me. Their god disappoints me. His followers disappoint me. Until you."

"I am not one of them."

"But you believe more passionately than any ten of them. And when you cast out a spirit, out the spirit goes. Nor did it come back again . . . easily."

Amon's words were making Flora angry, and she wasn't sure why. True, he made her feel like a curiosity piece, but she'd always been that. Maybe it was that he was denigrating people she looked up to, learned from—the Great God's followers at Essea. Maybe it was his implicit mockery of the Great God himself. Or maybe it was just the casual way he spoke of destroying a man's soul.

Amon continued. "I am glad you asked for leave and a place to pray. It would have disappointed me to find that your faith could not hold up under adversarial circumstances. I have always thought you stronger than that, and I am pleased to find that I was right."

"Is there ever a time you are not pleased with yourself?" Flora asked. "In the Westland they would warn you of hubris. They would say it displeases the gods."

Amon smirked. "Perhaps it does. *Those* gods. It matters, doesn't it?—what gods you align yourself with?"

"Indeed," Flora said, raising her wineglass and tilting her head. "Indeed it does."

  RACHEL STARR THOMSON

CHAPTER 3

Aurelius Florus Laurentinus arrived in the Holy City in a moderate show of pomp. His wife, Marah, accompanied him, along with a bustling cadre of servants. They put in an appearance at the temple immediately, making their presence known, smiling, gossiping, feeling out their standing with new and old.

Though his duties as governor had kept him in Bethabara for some time, Aurelius was good at this. A lifetime of practice in the shadow of father and grandfathers who were also good at it had made ingratiating himself second nature. He knew how to win favor without losing any of his own advantage. He let no hint of the crisis that had driven him here slip. Even when the whirling trumpets of the priests of Kimash alerted him to their entrance to the temple, he did not let his face show revulsion or fear.

The priests came in through the high east gate—the Dawn Gate, most sacred of the four temple gates. Even Aurelius knew it ought not to be used by any but the high priest of the Great God and the king of the Sacred Land, but no one in the temple seemed bothered by the breach. Just as no one batted an eye at the pagan altars and shrines lining the walls, or at the great altar being erected in the center of the outer court to Amon-Heth, a notable and frightening deity of the Southern Plains. The kings themselves had opened the temple to these alliances. And sacrifices to the Great God of the Holy People continued as they always had.

The priests of Kimash entered in an ecstatic frenzy. They wore long black robes, and their long hair streamed about their heads as they cavorted and slashed themselves with knives, spurting blood. They sang in high, affected voices as they tumbled over one another on their way to the inner court where their shrine was located. Their eyes had been painted with kohl and their cheeks streaked with blood.

Aurelius shuddered. The displays of the Hill People held no attraction for him. He could not see that the benefits of accessing Kimash's alleged power outweighed the loss of humanity associated with the deity's worship. Indeed, many of his most devoted seemed to become little more than beasts.

And then there were the killers—the black-robed assassins, their faces covered, their voices like ice. Only once had Aurelius ever seen one—in the court of the king, bearing a message from the Hill Country. He had never forgotten the chill he felt in the man's presence.

When Nadab the Trader came to him claiming that his household had been murdered in the night by Kimash's servants, he'd felt that chill again. He hardly even needed Nadab to describe the assassins.

The priests spilled past, and Aurelius backed away, pulling back the edge of his robe for fear that they would stumble into him and stain it. All eyes watched them go until they passed through the door of the inner court and disappeared behind its high walls.

Aurelius cleared his throat and turned his attention back to the man he was conversing with—an idol maker called Helchi.

"What do you think of this invasion of Kimash?" Aurelius asked, keeping his voice friendly and casual.

 RACHEL STARR THOMSON

"I don't care for their style of worship," Helchi said. But he gestured behind him to a shelf of small statues of the two-headed god, expertly fashioned in wood and bronze. "But they pay good money just like anyone else, and their high priest is a man of great influence at court—great and growing." He waggled bushy eyebrows. "The rank-and-file priests are just an irritation. Like all the Hill People."

Aurelius grunted his agreement. Long ago the Hill People had been a kingdom to reckon with, but in the last century their power had eroded until they were little more than a collection of hungry, ragged tribes, united by culture and language but more likely to war against each other than present any threat to the rest of the world.

"I am surprised to see them here," Aurelius said. "I knew the laws had grown lax, but . . ."

Helchi looked knowingly at him. "The high priest consecrated an altar to Kimash in the inner court six months ago, and since then the ancient ban on their presence in the temple has fallen out of effect. But the Great God reacted as he usually does—which is to say not at all."

Helchi laughed, but for some reason his words made Aurelius uneasy. Perhaps it was the near memory of Flora's last visit, with her always fervent devotion to the Great God—and her refusal, as half Hill Woman herself, to enter the temple of the god she loved. He was not a superstitious man, but it was hard not to be affected at least a little by Flora. Especially with Kol Abaddon haunting the wilderness near Bethabara and declaring his frightening visions of judgment to the people of the town. Aurelius had his hands full just keeping their fears calmed.

But if he'd thought the Great God's messengers were a problem, they were nothing to Kimash. Nadab's slaughtered household would cause not just holy fear, but panic. He had done all he could to contain the problem in Bethabara itself, but he knew rumors would leak soon.

Hence his coming here, to gain an audience with the king as soon as possible and attempt to obtain his help. Justice needed to be done, and quickly; the people needed to know they were safe. Without that, Aurelius feared unrest would turn into something worse. Thieves and killers would be emboldened; innocent people would be hurt. If things continued unchecked, revolt might begin to stir.

It didn't take much to kick the Holy People, with their gilded history of freedom, power, and divine protection, into revolt.

In the meantime, talking to Helchi could only help. The artisan was one of those men destined to climb any rank he inserted himself into—a man with eyes and ears everywhere, a disposition friendly enough to make friends and a mind shrewd enough to take advantage of them.

Low chanting, creating an eerie hum, filled the courtyard as the sun began to sink. Entering this time from the west gate came a procession of open-robed Southern priests, their eyes surrounded with black paint, bald heads glimmering, their hands carrying swinging censers. These walked calmly, almost too calmly, seeming to float over the ground as they made their way toward the half-finished altar of Amon-Heth.

Even as they did, small crowds of the People were gathering at the fountains near each gate to wash themselves for the evening sacrifice to the Great God. Aurelius spotted some of the Holy People's priests appearing in the doorways to the inner court, eyeing the faithful and the pouches of money they brought in lieu of blood sacrifices.

Overhead, the golden roof blazed with the light of the setting sun. Just as it had for centuries.

But truly, Aurelius mused, the temple of the Great God had changed. And with it, all Shalem. The Holy People had left their consecration to a single deity and thrown open the gates, quite literally, to the nations.

Aurelius thought he should be grateful for that. After all, he was a stranger himself, his ancestors having come from the Westland three

 Rachel Starr Thomson

generations before. A generation ago he would not have been allowed to enter the inner court, but he knew he would be welcomed if he tried to go in now.

He had never tried. He didn't know why. Respect for the People's history, perhaps. The kings of Shalem had begun welcoming other gods and alliances long ago, but the temple had been the last holdout—the last place in the city to cling to the ritual purity that once meant so much to this nation.

That they had lost that purity, so completely that the blood-spurting priests of Kimash could parade through the eastern gate and the temple courts without protest, saddened him somehow.

Helchi did not seem to share his scruples. He was pointing to various small idols in his market stall and giving a rundown of the strengths of each god and the practices of its worshippers. Curious and uncomfortable, Aurelius scanned the shelves for any sign of his own ancestral deities. Helchi noticed the shift in his attention.

"And what are you looking for, my fine governor?"

Aurelius smiled. "Not a Westlander in sight, I see."

Helchi grimaced. "The playboy deities of the west are not over-popular here. Not yet. Though they say the gods are moving east with sailors from across the sea. Soon I may be learning to carve features handsome as your own."

"You will do it well." Aurelius bent closer to examine the fine detail on a foot-tall statue of Amon-Heth—a weird, jackal-headed god carved of ebony, with a body that was too tall and too thin. "No other has your skill, Helchi."

The merchant beamed, though he tried not to show it. "A lifetime of practice, that is all. My grandfather was among the first to embrace the trade, back in the days when the priests of the Great God were still screaming apostasy."

"Was it the people themselves, then, who embraced the gods of strangers first? I had thought the priests led the way."

Helchi shrugged. "Who can say? Sometimes it seems as though change is in the air, and it happens all at once. The common people, the priests, the princes—history would say it was our King Balim, five generations back, who opened the doors to the nations. But he was not alone. The priests had already lost the books of the Great God long before then, and the covenant stones. And no one deposed him when he began to worship the strangers' gods."

Aurelius straightened and turned to face the temple court again, taking in the enormous paving stones, the fountains and pools, the sweeping walls. The wall separating inner and outer courts was nine feet tall and festooned with bronze and copper; and from within the inner court rose the highest of the temple structures: the sanctuary, with its soaring, golden-roofed spires. It alone remained sacred to the Great God—at least, last he had heard.

Balim's grandson of several generations removed was king now, and the question of other gods a settled one in his mind. Aurelius had once heard the prophet's warnings brought up in his presence. Beniah had waved his hand and dismissed the reports, his expression weary.

"Nothing but the ravings of a bitter, lonely man," he said. "I did all I could for his family, but he will not forgive what happened to them. He takes out his anger by threatening doom upon us all. The warnings will cease with his passing."

"A passing you might aid," a powerful merchant had suggested. "The man is a scourge, and some of his teachings interfere with our trade. Certainly he blights the happiness of your subjects."

But Beniah would not hear of it. "The man has suffered more than most already. I will not make his suffering worse. Let the people listen to him if they will. If it were not him, it would be some other

     RACHEL STARR THOMSON

mangy teacher to tickle their ears. They are hungry for stories and scares, that is all."

Aurelius wondered if the king still felt the same way. Tensions had heated considerably since that conversation. But then—it had been some weeks since Kol Abaddon last appeared in Bethabara, or even since Aurelius had heard reports of his howling in the wilderness.

Perhaps the day Beniah waited for had come, and the prophet had died somewhere out in the lonely desert—released from his torment at last.

As the time for evening sacrifices approached, the crowds in the temple courts thickened—not because most were devout, but because rituals were rituals, and now was the best time for traffic and gossip and merchandising. Helchi left Aurelius's side with an apology to attend to several interested customers, and the governor of Bethabara tried to shake off the malaise that had suddenly come over him.

Marah appeared at his side—she had been with a group of women not far away. She took his arm.

"Shall we stay for the sacrifices, husband?" she asked.

Aurelius shook his head. "I think not. I for one am weary from the journey."

Marah looked around and wrinkled her nose. "And overwhelmed by choice. Even if we were to stay for the sacrifice, whose sacrifice would we attend?"

He gave her a sharp look, but he could not tell from her expression if she spoke lightly or if she was truly bothered by this. Marah's family was as modern and metropolitan as they came, and yet, they were of the Holy People—of the priestly line, in fact.

He wondered if this circus bothered her like it was unexpectedly bothering him.

He set his hand over hers and steered her toward the south gate. A chariot waited to bear them to their lodging on the wealthy north side of the city, on the mountain slopes where country estates stood far from the squalor of the city proper. Their steward had been alerted of their coming; all would be ready for them.

Helchi popped up by Aurelius's elbow, having haggled his way nearly out the gate with a customer. "Now's the time to take an interest in Kimash," he said, his voice conspiratorially low. "If ever a god was on the ascendant, it's now."

"Can you tell me why?" Aurelius asked.

"Marriage, my friend," Helchi said, fingering his nose with a smirk. "Marriage."

Aurelius opened his mouth to ask further questions, but fanfare blaring from the east gate interrupted him. Helchi slapped him on the back and shouted, "It's the king!"

Marah whispered in his ear, "I'll meet you outside," and slipped away.

Through the Dawn Gate processed a well-dressed retinue of servants and guards, followed by the king's family—two wives and eight sons, from a toddling three-year-old to strapping young men. Two of the boys, Aurelius knew, were recently motherless. Beniah's favored wife had died less than a year ago of a wasting disease.

Beniah himself entered last, accompanied by a man on either side: to his right the son of the Great God's high priest, Jeshiel, and to his left, the dark figure Aurelius recognized as the high priest of Kimash.

The high priest of Kimash was a tall, swarthy man. His black hair fell in ringlets down to the middle of his back. He wore a long black robe and rings on all his fingers. Like the others, his face was painted, his eyes darkened by kohl. Unlike the Southern priests, the priests of Kimash also reddened their cheeks and lips with blood, and the backs

     RACHEL STARR THOMSON

of their arms, hands, and necks bore tattoos: pictures indicating role and rank; words indicating spells, curses, and protections in the language of the Hill People.

Aurelius knew the high priest immediately, though he had never met him and did not know his name. He had never forgotten a brief glimpse of the man's forebear—dressed and tattooed identically to this man—when he was a child and he and his father were visiting Flora's mother in the Hill Country. As a boy his soul had wrestled between a wild desire to mock the man—with his womanish appearance and strange speech—and a deep terror of him.

This incarnation of Kimash's highest-ranking servant inspired much the same feelings. As the procession passed, the high priest paused. His eyes met Aurelius's for an instant, and then he continued on. So Aurelius was staring at him, and got a detailed look at the pattern embroidered all down the back of the man's long black cassock: the detailed figure—head, back, and tail—of a dragon.

Helchi was prattling on about something; Aurelius had ceased to listen. He watched as the royal procession passed into the sanctuary, where the king would offer his own sacrifice to the Great God as his forebears had done for hundreds of years. But how strange the company he kept!

He turned once more to go, saying good-bye to Helchi, when a servant tapped him on the shoulder. He turned to see a man dressed in the king's livery.

"Greetings, Aurelius," the man said, bowing his head. "His highness saw you on his way and regrets that he could not stop to greet you himself. He would like to see you at his table tomorrow."

"I will be there," Aurelius said.

CHAPTER 4

Flora did not walk to prayer first thing in the evening after being released from Amon's company—she paraded there. It was not easy to parade all by oneself, but she managed it, with four bewildered guards trudging behind her. If Amon was going to insist that she dress like the queen of Sheba, she at least would make a public spectacle of herself in a way that counted.

How it counted, she wasn't entirely sure. The parade itself was meant as something of a demonstration of the Great God's superiority, a visible rebuke of everyone else in the camp for worshipping inferior spirits that barely deserved the name "gods." Perhaps she hoped it would awaken someone to seeking a better faith.

By the time she dropped to her knees in her chosen spot, though—beside a large limestone rock under two crossed palm trees by the pool of water—she was fairly sure she ought to repent. One didn't flounce into the Great God's presence, and one didn't pray so that other people would see. In Essea they taught that prayer should be solitary, secluded, a secret. True enough that everyone in the community knew everyone else was at prayer and when, but you couldn't help that when everybody was doing the same thing. They still tried to be circumspect about it.

Praying in a public place, in a scarlet dress, under guard, was not circumspect in any way, and Flora had not exactly helped that by the manner in which she chose the spot and walked to it.

On her knees in the dust, not caring that the dress was getting dirty already, Flora closed her eyes, leaned against the rock with her hands folded, and felt herself fall apart on the inside.

What was she doing?

What was she supposed to say?

Here I am, God. You threw me out of your presence, but I am back anyway. I intend to keep coming back, if only to rub your enemies' faces in it, until the day you strike me dead.

She couldn't pray that.

But she couldn't pray anything else either.

So she spent twenty minutes or so on her knees staring at the rock, listening to the palm branches rustle overhead as the sun began to sink over the desert and turn the shades of the limestone from dull tan to bright white, streaked with veins of yellow and pale green, and then brightening to blue as the sun sank even lower.

She finally got off her knees, using the rock to help herself. Her legs had fallen asleep and her joints ached, and she picked her way carefully back through the tents to the one Amon had appointed for her.

When she got back inside, she noted that he'd had it furnished while she was away. Apparently her promotion from prisoner to guest entailed more than just meals with the master and a place to pray. Rugs had been rolled out across the hard dirt and the bigger rocks cleared away from beneath them and stacked in a corner. An actual bed had replaced the mat, and a washbasin stood beside it with a clay pitcher of water. There were, as well, enough curtains to create a private room on one side and a small chair where she could sit. Along with all of this, she noted the presence of a sandalwood chest where she presumed more clothing awaited, and a bowl of dates should she grow hungry.

None of the furnishings were elaborate or ostentatious, but they were hospitable and more than adequate for a caravan.

She also noticed, with an unhappy glare at the tent side, that the image of Kimash remained.

An errant thought flew through her mind—wondering if Kimash was more interested in her prayers than the Great God seemed to be.

He was the god of her people, after all.

She didn't mean anything by the thought—hadn't even called it up through any sort of meditation. It went running through her head without permission or forethought, and it left behind it a darkness.

But it brought her childhood rushing back. The shrine behind her mother's house. The wicked men who came in and out. The idol that watched her with tangible hunger.

Almost without meaning to, she began to pray one of the old ritual prayers for protection that she had learned in Essea. The words spilled out of her mouth in a rush, growing louder and more forceful as they came.

She finished the prayer and stood staring up at the image of Kimash, breathing hard.

It stared back.

She turned on her heel and left the tent. Guards rushed after her. She ignored them.

She had been here a week, but something had changed. The image seemed to see her now.

She could not stay there another minute.

Nadab the Trader felt the weariness in every bone as he and his servant crested a hill of sand and looked out over a long stretch of dunes and valleys leading away to the east. The hot sun battered down and called up waves of heat from the horizon.

"We must cease our journeying and find shade," Lethem fretted. "It is not safe, my lord."

"We should press on," Nadab said, but he heard the lackluster tone of his own voice and knew he had lost the argument. His fear of Kimash's assassins had grown less potent with each day's distance from Bethabara, and though it was still strong, it was no longer enough to prevail over his exhausted body.

Besides, Lethem was right. It was madness to ride in the heat of the sun over such a featureless landscape.

He sighed as his servant pulled his horse to a halt and reached for its reins. "There is shade to the south," Lethem said. "I see a great rock."

Nadab looked but could see nothing but the waving heat. "You see a mirage."

"No, indeed, my lord, the rock is there."

This time, when he peered a little harder, Nadab thought perhaps he could make it out too. At least he thought he saw a dark patch on the sand—the shade cast by the rock, and their present help. Lethem was tugging at his own reins now, guiding his horse's head away and toward the south.

"Come," he said. "Soon we will cover our heads and find rest to our bones."

   RACHEL STARR THOMSON

"Not too much rest," Nadab said sharply. "Kimash must know we are not failing him."

The servant grumbled something he could not hear, and when he partially turned, Nadab saw tears running down his face. The assassins had slaughtered Lethem's family and close friends. He did not complain, but his heart must be ready to fail him for the pain.

"Kimash will have to allow us to be human," Lethem said. "No one has ever shown so much dedication in reaching the east."

Nadab thought for a moment before he spoke the words. "I am sorry. For all you have lost."

His servant, leading both horses, did not look back. But Nadab heard his reply.

"It was a terrible thing. But you did not do it. I curse Kimash, not you."

Nadab shuddered. "Not too loud."

This time Lethem did cast a glance back, unashamed of the tears on his sun-weathered cheeks. "I care not if he hears me. I wish he had killed me with all the others. You are guiltless, my lord; the god cannot accuse you of a disrespectful word."

Nadab did not point out that every slaughtered man and woman had been innocent; it had been Nadab's sin of losing his daughter that brought their deaths upon them in the night. Kimash did not seem to care much for individual justice.

Perhaps, came a thought through his mind, the People had given up more than they realized when they ceased their single devotion to the Great God and began to seek the idols of the nations alongside him.

In the sun and the sand distance was not easily gauged, but not much ground had slipped away from beneath the horse hooves before they entered the shade of the great rock. The immediate drop in temperature brought relief Nadab hadn't known he needed. His eyes, too, eased as the darkness came over them, and he blinked away sun spots as his horse ambled forward.

His servant stopped so abruptly the horse bumped into his back. Too weary and too heart-sore to curse him, Nadab just looked up.

He saw the bandits huddled against the rock, cruel smiles greeting his arrival, for only an instant before they struck.

CHAPTER 5

Rechab Nadab's daughter wavered between bewilderment and elation as her journey south progressed. Only days ago she had been a runaway with no real hope or resources, only a tenuous plan to find some market town on the borders of the Southern Plains where she could make a life for herself as a merchantwoman.

That plan remained her intention. But the path to get there had marvelously transformed. In lending Rechab her name, Flora had given her wonders.

As the representative of Flora Laurentii, Rechab was surrounded now by a devoted cadre of servants, bodyguards, and guides who arose early in the morning without any need of command and readied the entire caravan for the journey. They pulled down tents, saddled camels, readied skins of water and wine.

Breakfast appeared in her luxurious tents, full and delicious. By the time she finished it, a camel had been made ready with veiled litter, and she rode in the luxury she had once seen Flora ensconced in on the way to the religious community of Essea.

And her religion—that was the other change. Rechab had stepped into Flora's footsteps here too, leading the caravan in a prayer of thanks every day and being sure to pray alone at intervals throughout the hours. At first she had only intended to do so once a day—in Flora's name, for the sake of maintaining a normal schedule for the entourage, and in order to honor her own newfound commitment to the Great God of her ancestors. But as the hours for prayer came around, she found herself using all three in the day, just as Flora always did. Every time she went to prayer she found herself strengthened in spirit, feeling as though she had just spent time with a friend—even though, in the moment, prayer seemed nothing more than the awkward muttering of words that felt unnatural in her mouth.

She was still very new to this, but she decided that the Great God must be pleased with her attempts. Why else did she feel so encouraged after seeking him?

The day passed like the days before it—in riding over the desert sands, resting in the hottest part of the day, prayer, the pleasant sounds and sights of the caravan on the move. For once, she felt no fear. There was no indication of anyone pursuing them, and she found she could rest in the knowledge that Flora's great wealth and influence were at her disposal.

They set up camp in a shallow green valley intersected by a river and shaded by palms and acacias that flourished by the water. Aaron, functioning as her right-hand man, cheerfully told her about the nearby villages and the bustling fishing trade here, as well as the presence of several copper mines in the gentle hills. Flora sometimes did trade with them, though she did not often come down here herself. Most often she sent trusted servants to transact business for her while she remained cloistered in Essea.

With Aaron pontificating by her side, Rechab wandered through the camp as it rose on poles and ropes all around her. A breeze off the river waved palm fronds and carried the scent of desert orchids. The

     RACHEL STARR THOMSON

camels, picketed off to one side and carefully guarded, chewed their cud contentedly.

Aaron stopped talking and frowned at a slight commotion on the other end of the camp.

"What is it?" Rechab asked, turning. Her view was blocked by the broad shoulders and backs of her own servants—four men who had formed a guarding wall.

"Strangers," Aaron said. "You should stay out of sight, at least until we know who they are."

Rechab nodded agreement, and Aaron led her to Flora's luxurious tent. She took her seat amongst the silk cushions in one of the smaller chambers toward the back of the tent, leaving the larger receiving room empty. She strained her ears to hear any of the conversation outside, but the tent walls muffled every sound, and the visitors were too far away anyway. Most likely it was nothing.

Aaron appeared moments later, still frowning. "They wish to speak with Flora," he said.

Rechab blinked. "Well, they can't."

To her shock, Aaron shook his head and said, "I think they should. I think you should veil yourself and speak with them."

"What? Why? Who are they, Aaron?"

"Better that they tell you that for themselves. They do not know Mistress Flora; veil yourself and they will not recognize you."

Alarm was rising in her. "Aaron, I can't speak on Flora's behalf."

"Then just *listen* on her behalf."

From the expression on his face, she could see she would get nowhere arguing. Stubborn as the mules he bred, she thought. But why would he insist on this?

"I'm not Flora," she offered as one last resistance.

His jaw tightened. "But she put you in her place. She would want you to listen. Even to speak for her, if you are moved to do so."

She sighed. "Very well. Bring them in. But give me a few minutes."

He nodded and left. Muttering to herself, she veiled her face and figure and released another sigh. What was she doing? What was she even *thinking*? What was Aaron thinking? Flora's identity was just a disguise meant to take her south, not a license to act for her. Right?

Seated in the midst of a pile of ornate cushions, she straightened her back and veil and took a deep breath, then clasped her hands in her lap and waited for the strangers to be admitted.

Aaron did not keep her waiting long. Scant moments after she had prepared herself, the curtained doors parted and he led in three souls so wretched that Rechab had to stop herself from gasping aloud.

The strangers were a man and two women. The man's back was hunched and his face deeply lined; though he looked a hundred, she suspected he was much younger than the ravages on his body indicated. His clothes were in tatters, and he wore no shoes. Of the women, both were of an age likewise impossible to determine. One had a face marred by burn scars covering half of her face from forehead to chin. A strip of cloth wrapped around her head covered one eye; Rechab suspected it was missing, but she could not tell. The other woman had white hair and hands that shook. Like the man, both wore rags and went barefoot.

Wrestling between revulsion and compassion, she wondered why on earth Aaron had brought them to her. She had been expecting a trader or an emissary from the village, someone whose requests she would have to resist. Instead, she heard herself opening the conversation with the words, "What can I do for you?"

Before they even spoke she had made up her mind to feed and clothe them before they went away. Flora would want her to do so.

 RACHEL STARR THOMSON

The man spoke in a sere voice. "If you please, Mistress," he said, "we come seeking justice."

It was not what she expected to hear. Food, clothing, mercy, yes. But justice?

"Tell me your story," she said.

Instead, he continued, "We have heard of Flora Infortunatia's good heart and that you will not abide cruelty. We want you to advocate for us. It's our last hope, Mistress."

She swallowed hard and repeated, "Tell me your story. I will listen."

"We are only three among many whose stories are the same," the man said. "We are villagers, of the mining town of Nachush on the south side of the river. For generations our families fished here—we are honest folk. But the mines have changed everything."

The women nodded, and Rechab steeled herself for what she knew was to come. Had she not seen hints of it for years, as she hovered around her father's business dealings? Whoever controlled mines gained wealth, and with wealth power. At first they were a boon to all in a given region, but then the power began to be mismanaged, and soon the people became little more than slaves under the thumb of the mine masters. If they tried to bring grievances to the village court of elders, their cause was overcome by bribes and corruption.

She closed her eyes as the man indeed told just that story—with a merchant called Azeda the worst of the offenders. Originally the mines had been controlled by three men, but two had died in "accidents" laid to Azeda's account. No justice had been done. And in his greed for power and wealth, Azeda had conscripted every villager into working for him, then paid them only the barest minimum needed to survive.

"We starve," the man said, "and he sells us food on credit, then takes our children into slavery to pay our debts. None will stand against him. Truly, Azeda's wickedness is killing us all. You see me here with my sisters—both have been widowed by the mines. The deaths are Azeda's fault, for he does nothing to safeguard his workers, but he refuses responsibility and will make no restitution according to the law. Nor does he respect the year of release. It has been three years since our children's terms of slavery were up, but he will not release them. The village elders are under his thumb, either afraid or corrupted. We have no recourse, and without help, we will die."

She wanted to say, Why come to me? What do you think I can do?

But the man continued.

"We have come to you," he said, "because we have heard of Flora Laurentii the Devout, and we know that you fear God and care for the poor. We have heard how you stand against injustice. We need you to help us now."

How could she say no?

Flora's voice would not have trembled, so Rechab forced herself to keep hers steady, to sound confident even as she asked, "But what can I do?"

Aaron, lingering in the wings, spoke. "Use your wealth," he said. "This Azeda will speak the language of money. Use it to force him to do right by these people. To honor the laws of the Great God."

She shot him a look, but he went on, turning to the poor beggars. "Go now," he said. "Rest assured that Flora will help you. You have come to the right place."

Bowing and scraping, expressing their gratitude in pitiful terms, the beggars vanished and left Rechab feeling like she couldn't breathe.

Aaron turned to her immediately, his dark eyes flashing with anger and passion. She drew back, thinking he was angry with her, but his words quickly revealed that his anger had a different object.

"I have known many like this Azeda," he said. "They enslave and

     RACHEL STARR THOMSON

abuse, and no one stops them. Praise the Great God for sending these beggars to you!"

Rechab's heart sank as Aaron paced. "I will go out as your emissary and call Azeda and the elders into an audience," he said. "They will agree to meet with you."

"They will?"

"Of course they will. You are Flora Laurentii. They do not dare deny you. Among merchants, Flora is a powerful woman."

Rechab's mouth gaped as she tried to answer. Of course Aaron was right—they had no choice but to try to do something. At least, they had no choice *now*. Her heart had sunk down to her feet, and she tried to pull it back up by picturing the beggars and rousing her fury at the injustices they had faced—or at the very least rousing enough compassion to make her feel stronger.

She suspected Flora would be better at the compassion, and far better at the fury. Right now all she felt was fear.

Aaron seemed to see that, and his tone changed—becoming reassuring, the voice of a friend.

"You are up to this challenge, Rechab," he said. "You only need ask what Mistress Flora would do. Perhaps they will not even oppose you overmuch. Perhaps the men who control this village will see the benefit to them and change their ways without a fight."

"How often does *that* happen?" Rechab asked.

Aaron shrugged. "Money is powerful. More powerful than you know. It can even make bad men good . . . for a while."

"Then it is the greatest power in the universe," Rechab muttered. She pulled her veil away from her face and tried to calm her sickened stomach. She ought to be overfamiliar with the power of money, but she had always tried just to serve her father and not to become too embroiled in the realities of what his trade did to him and to others.

Aaron was looking at her in a way that made her feel uncomfortable. She cleared her throat and ducked her eyes, and he seemed to catch himself—he turned and stumbled over his words.

"I will make all the arrangements," he said. "If the Great God smiles on us, they will meet with you before evening falls."

She wanted to grab his sleeve and pull him back. "I don't know what I'm doing, Aaron!"

He turned back and smiled. It was a handsome smile, confident and reassuring even if he was getting her into trouble. "You will do fine. Just ask yourself what the mistress would do."

The mistress, Rechab thought as Aaron exited the shade of the tent into the glaring sun, would have swept imperiously into the village and turned the whole place upside-down by force of her personality. But Rechab did not have Flora's personality, even if she was wearing her name. Nor did she have her remarkably quick mind and ability to keep control of a situation.

"Aaron!" she called, panicked. He ducked back inside immediately, and now his eyes were warm and comforting—she felt embraced by his gaze. His tone, too, had softened.

"You don't need to be afraid," he said.

Her eyes pleaded with him. "I only took Flora's name so that I could start over," she said.

"And what better way to do it than this? By accepting the gifts the mistress has given you and becoming the champion she would be? You are more than a runaway, Rechab. It was you Flora chose to manage her affairs in Bethabara, and you did a fine job of it. You have helped to manage your father's business for many years. You can do this."

She nodded, took a deep breath, and forced down another wave of

 RACHEL STARR THOMSON

panic. That had all been different. That had all been serving beer and wine and charming crowds of men into waiting patiently. Lives had not hung in the balance. Least of all her own.

Just what *would* happen if anyone found out the truth? That she was not Flora Laurentii, but was using Flora's name and influence and even her money to bluff her way through the world until she could find a safe place to start life over, far away from her father and his terrifying designs for her?

Aaron ducked outside, leaving her alone, and she could hear him on the other side of the tent wall, giving orders. A mule boy he might be, but he was a natural leader, and no one among Flora's retinue seemed to mind that he had taken charge. There was remarkably little competition among them, just as there was remarkably little protest to Rechab's presence. In the past she would have assumed they did not care who was in charge so long as they were paid, but it went deeper than that. These were good men, deeply loyal to one another and to the mistress they loved and honored. They were acting on the orders of that mistress now, and so they treated Rechab with the same loyalty and care. She was grateful to them all.

Standing, she closed her eyes to entreat the Great God's care. She hoped he saw what she was doing and approved of it. Did not the old laws entreat the People to care for the poor and fight for the oppressed? Though she knew only snatches of the Great God's law—the books of law had been lost long ago, so that only scattered teachings from the priests survived—she was sure of those precepts. The wild prophet, Kol Abaddon, had often harangued against the People's failure to keep them.

God willing, she would not add to that failure.

Jonah bar Kebna, the Teacher of Essea, called the pilgrims to prayer with fear.

How many times had they prayed since sending Flora away? How many times had they gone through the motions, the rituals, the bowing and chanting and lighting of incense? And every time there had been no response, no presence of the Great God in their midst.

As it would be again. Yet again, all there would be to answer them was emptiness.

This made the Teacher tremble, and he did not bother to hide it.

Why pretend all was well when the truth was the terrible opposite?

In the thirty years since he and his brother had founded this community in the desert, he had studied the fragments that could be found of the ancient laws and the history of the Holy People, and he had taught the brothers and sisters who came and joined them: taught them of the Great God and his righteous laws, taught them of the covenant with the Holy People and how the Holy People had broken it. He taught them of the temple in Shalem and how it had once been the sanctuary of the Great God on earth, designed according to blueprints given directly from heaven, but how the People had turned the temple into a mockery by inviting other gods into its adulterous courts, and how the presence of the Great God had ceased to be felt there and how this portended something terrible.

But he had also taught that the People had hope, for the presence of the Great God could still be found in their prayers, there in Essea, and among other clusters of the faithful devout. Though the priests were corrupted, the Teacher and others like him had stepped into their place as bearers of the covenant and so stood in the gap for the whole nation.

But now the Great God had left them too.

How was it possible?

How could it be that in driving one woman away—a foreigner, not even allowed into the temple, the illegitimate child of a power-grabbing Westlander and an idol-worshipping Hill Woman—he had driven away the presence of the Great God himself?

The long hall lay before him, its interior dim with the light of burning incense. The faithful came in one by one and bowed their faces to the ground, row after row dressed in white and prostrate before him as though it was to him they bowed.

As though he could give them hope.

He could give them nothing.

Within him, something snapped.

To his own shock, he heard his voice bark out into the quiet of their prayers—into the stillness that was meant to be reverence and private communion.

"Get up!" he said. "Get up, all of you!"

Confused, the brothers and sisters of Essea shuffled to an upright position. A few stood on their feet.

 Rachel Starr Thomson

"All of you," the Teacher repeated, impatient now.

This was enough. No more farce. They would not do as the priests in the temple had done—continuing in empty ritual while the Presence had gone.

"Can you not feel it?" the Teacher asked.

He knew from their faces that they could. He saw fear in their eyes—fear, and some relief as he spoke. Relief that the truth was being acknowledged.

"The Great God has left us. His eye no longer looks on our prayers. We must not go on pretending that nothing has changed. My friends, I have sinned."

His voice broke. He wanted to weep. Perhaps to panic. He kept his voice as steady as he could.

"I betrayed the young girl who sought shelter here, and I sent away Flora Laurentii—one of our own. One who was more righteous than I. Somehow, with her going, the Great God has also gone. Perhaps my sin of injustice drove him away."

"What do we do?" someone asked.

He shook his head, but ideas were coming. "We pray. We beg. We fast. Not prayers as usual. We must repent. We must acknowledge the wrong and the absence and plead with the Great God to return to us before it is too late."

His eyes filled up with tears.

"We have long been the last stay between the People and judgment. Kol Abaddon long ago began to prophesy that judgment would come. My friends, I do not know if we can stop it. But I know we are not innocent. I am not innocent."

Others began to talk amongst themselves, and some to weep. He heard agreement and some discussion.

Then one of his acolytes, still on his knees in the front of the room, tore his garment. The sound of the rip could be heard to the ends of the long hall. Like a trumpet blast, it called the faithful to repentance.

The weeping and wailing began in earnest, and the Teacher took hold of his own white garment and tore it, from the neck to the hem. He turned himself so that his back was to the community he had led so long, and broken, he lowered his face to the earth and began to weep.

With all his heart he wished the Great God to hear and answer.

But as he wept, it seemed to him that his tears fell into a great emptiness, and no answer nor echo returned.

He did not know how many minutes or hours passed before he became aware that something was different.

He raised his head to see six young men standing in their midst, dressed in traveling clothes and looking around them in confusion and distress.

"Teacher, we are home," said one, "and grieved to find things in such a state. What has happened to drive all of Essea to its knees in such a fashion?"

He knew these six. Disciples who had been on a long journey. When last they were here in the community's sanctuary, Essea had been the heart of devout worship of the Great God, blessed with his presence and thriving, with new acolytes flooding in and hope of change in the air.

The home they found now, two years later, was very different indeed.

The Teacher groaned deeply as he rose. His knees and legs and back ached from hours spent kneeling, seeking the return of the Great God's presence. Even before calling for this repentance, he had gone days already without eating or drinking, and he felt the weakness of it.

The great men of old, the prophets and servants of the Great God, had fasted forty days and more with neither food nor water. But the presence of the Great God had fed and watered them, sustaining them with spiritual food and drink that empowered even their bodies.

The Teacher could claim no such presence and no such feeding. Ashamed though he was to admit it, he would not pretend to greater holiness than he now knew himself to possess. He was not a great prophet, and Essea was no longer the sanctuary of the Great God.

They could only beg him to forgive them and return.

"Terrible things have befallen us, my sons," the Teacher said as he stood on legs that wanted nothing but to collapse beneath him. He saw the worry in their faces, but they stayed on their knees, not shaming him by running to his rescue as though he were a helpless old man.

The Teacher of Essea was not old, though he was quickly beginning to feel that he was obsolete. Indeed, he was younger than Kol Abaddon.

Not many in the Sacred Land knew how old or young Kol Abaddon was.

The Teacher knew many things that others did not. And yet he himself remained an enigma to most. Perhaps even to himself, he reflected.

Pah. He was wasting time feeling sorry for himself when these young men needed his welcome and his guidance—when the whole community needed the Great God, and the Sacred Land needed repentance. If he was truly the spiritual leader of the land, it was no wonder they were all in such deep trouble.

"I welcome you home," the Teacher said. "I am sorry there are not better tidings for you to come home to. You may join us in mourning and fasting, or leave us again, as you wish."

"We have traveled many miles to be with you again," the oldest of the six said. "We would not leave you now for any reason. But tell us, Great Teacher—what has happened?"

The Teacher shuddered. "Do not call me that, I pray you," he said. "I am not great. Not a great teacher, not even a great man. You wonder what has happened? The Great God's presence has abandoned us. We have defiled the last pure sanctuary in the Sacred Land. My sons, I have defiled it."

They did not hide their dismay. "But how? Surely the Great God will be merciful!"

"We seek his mercy," the Teacher said. "But I cannot say we have yet found it. We committed a grievous sin, my sons."

His eyes filled with tears, grief his body was far too weak to hold back even for the sake of leadership. Besides, what did it matter if these boys saw him cry? If they witnessed the true brokenness of his soul? A broken soul might be the best thing any of the People could wish for at this juncture in history—here, at the precipice of the Great God's judgment. Had not Kol Abaddon preached for years that the People must turn and repent? But what repentance ever came without brokenness and pain?

Of both, the Teacher had a surplus now.

"In my arrogance and in fear, I drove out two who sought protection here," the Teacher said. "One of them was our own Flora Laurentii. She is gone, and with her, the presence of the Great God."

The young men exchanged glances, clearly troubled. Compassion strained in their voices and eyes as they addressed him again.

"Perhaps the Great God has offered you a chance to redeem yourself," the leader said. "For another has come in need of refuge."

The Teacher lifted his eyes, startled. He had recognized no stranger among them. Nor did he now.

     Rachel Starr Thomson

"We have brought him here," the young man continued. "But he could not seek audience with us. We left him in one of the huts. In truth, Teacher, he is on the point of death."

"Who is he?" the Teacher asked, head swimming.

"We do not know. We found him among the dunes, left for dead. Bandits, no doubt. Another man traveled with him, but we could do nothing for him but bury his body away from the ravages of the sun and the buzzards."

"Bless you," the Teacher murmured. "Bless your good hearts. Take me to this newcomer. Of course we will do all we can for him."

His eyes and voice grew stern. "But we must not leave off our prayers and fastings. If you will stay, you will join us in this."

"Of course," said the leader of the young men again. "We came home to seek the Great God. So seek him we shall, no matter what he asks of us."

The Teacher's thoughts whirled as the young men led him to the hut where they and the community guards had already taken their rescued stranger. As soon as the Teacher pushed aside the skin that served as a door, he was hit by the smell of infection and the buzzing of flies. One of the young men dashed inside and began to swat the flies away.

"We did all we could for him, but infection has set in despite our best efforts. All we had to treat him was wine and bandages torn from our own clothing."

"Where was he?" the Teacher asked, inspecting the man. The stranger was large, broad-shouldered, probably intimidating when in health. But his face was white as ash, his breath a rasp. He showed no sign of awareness. Bandages wrapped around his midsection seeped blood.

"He will need the bandages changed and his wounds cleansed

again," the Teacher said. He laid a hand on the man's forehead—burning. "I will set the sisters to keeping him cool and as comfortable as possible, and we will have a small group cease their prayers of repentance and pray instead for this man's healing."

The chief of the young men bowed reverently. "You are good, Teacher. I think this is as the Great God would have it."

"Where did you find him?" the Teacher asked him again.

"In the dunes two days west of Essea. Left to die, as we said. He lay in the shadow of a rock, or the sun would have killed him before ever we reached him. He has not spoken, but we think it had been a day since the attack. No more."

The Teacher frowned, still examining the stranger. Something about his features was familiar—but he could not say why. He wondered if, rather than an innocent traveler attacked by bandits, this man had been one of the thieves himself. Who else would travel through such a wasteland? Most travelers took more hospitable routes to their destinations; the dunes were a hiding place for bandits who did not wish to be tracked between their raids.

It did not matter, he decided. Any man on the verge of death deserved attention.

And perhaps, as the young men had suggested, the Great God had sent this stranger so that the community might redeem themselves for sending—

He froze midthought.

Yes, he had seen the man's features before. But in a very different face.

"His daughter's face," he murmured.

"Did you say something?" one of the young men asked.

The Teacher waved his hand. "I said nothing of import. You are

RACHEL STARR THOMSON

newly arrived. Go and tend to yourselves, and send some of the faithful to me here. I will set the community to work at healing our strange friend."

But he was not a stranger.

The Teacher was sure of it. This was Nadab the Trader, the father of Rechab the runaway. Almost certainly seeking her.

And just as certainly sent here by God. This could not be coincidence.

He leaned close to the unconscious man, ignoring the smell of rot, and said in his ear, "I do not know the Great God's purposes in this, my friend. But I will declare my purpose to you: if it can be done, we will see you well again. Essea will not fail you as we failed your child. I promise you that."

CHAPTER 7

The town of Nachush—a bustling settlement, nearly a city—nestled in the valley at the foot of three hills where copper and tin—bronze—were present in rich veins. A languid river flowed nearby. Pillars of smoke rose from the smelting fires at the mouth of the mines, six of them wavering in the still air, and the clang of men at work carried into the valley. A thick adobe wall ringed the town, and it was to its gates—the traditional seat of judgment—that Aaron led Rechab, riding on a white mule.

Clusters of men and women had gathered on either side of the gate, and all eyes turned to regard Rechab curiously as she and Aaron rode up. Their chatter and jostling neither ceased nor quieted, but they parted to make room, and as she dismounted, Rechab recognized the elders: six aged men, sporting long beards and elaborate turbans, gathered within the thick gates themselves.

With them stood a large, thickly muscled man with a dark beard and darker eyes, dressed in rich silks. Even without speaking a word, the elders deferred to his presence.

Azeda.

Panic gripped her stomach again as she realized she didn't know what to do first, but Aaron solved her problem by offering her his hand. Grasping at any comforting distraction, her mind chose this moment to notice that Aaron, like the elders, was dressed in silks and wore a rich turban, making himself look like a vizier, or perhaps a prince—and increasing his appeal by about ten times. He had washed too.

She took his hand, fingers trembling. She straightened her back as Aaron led her into the council meeting.

One of the elders, an especially wide man with a gap-toothed smile, bowed and greeted her. "The famed Flora Laurentii! We welcome you!"

Rechab nodded and answered, "I thank you for the warmth of your greeting, and for agreeing to meet with me today."

She felt glad of her instincts. She did at least know how to comport herself well. If only she could reign her mind in—it was now reflecting on the greeting and whether anyone ever called Flora "Unlucky" to her face or only behind her back.

The other men bowed in greeting and formed a semicircle with Rechab at the center. Aaron bowed and released her hand, gesturing for her to sit. She had to twist her head around to see that there was indeed a chair there, and she sank down gratefully—hoping the action looked graceful and not like she was about to lose control of her legs. The latter was the more true.

Had she been a worshipper of the many gods of the nations, she would have thanked all of them for gifting mankind with the art of weaving, so that they could create veils that hid her face while still allowing her to see out. Since she was not, she silently thanked the Great God and cleared her throat as quietly as she could.

The men were waiting for her to speak.

While her mind froze, Aaron took the lead.

"We thank you for assembling," he said. "Your fine mines have

 RACHEL STARR THOMSON

drawn my mistress's interest. She seeks to expand her holdings, as you know . . ."

"Our mines are not for sale," the man she knew to be Azeda said. Rechab looked him in the face and was shaken by the hardness of his eyes. "The mines belong to me," he stated. "They are not for sale."

Aaron might have continued, but Rechab found her own voice. She and Aaron had already crafted an answer. "I do not wish to buy your mines," she said. "You seem too fine a businessman to think I could make you an offer worth more than the mines themselves will be to you and your family in the years to come. No, the holdings of which my servant speaks are those of alliance, not of land. As you know, my own mines are far to the east and north of here. I wish to bring my business west. You will have valuable connections here, men to whom I can sell. And I can offer you the same in the north and east. Allow me to send you my wares, and you may keep a percentage of the selling price."

"Bah," the large man said. The elders shifted with discomfort at his disdain, but no one corrected it. "You are competition. You mine copper and iron; we mine bronze. There is no profit to us in selling your wares instead of our own."

Aaron and Rechab exchanged a glance. She drew in a deep breath— she knew the words about to cross her lips had never crossed Flora's. But Aaron had assured her it was all right.

"You would be right," she said, "were it not that I have come into new wealth. I can offer you gold, and that is something you cannot mine here, nor can you sell anything you own for even a quarter of the price."

She saw the change come over the man's face, and the faces of the elders as well. She knew the change for what it was—the ugly greed and sudden hope, mingled, that Mammon always inspired in men.

"The Westlanders are greedy for gold," one of the elders said, nudging Azeda. "They say their king wishes to pave his roads with it.

They pay generously."

Azeda snorted, but his eyes stayed riveted on Rechab. "Gold," he said. "A vein . . . small quantities . . ."

Aware that she was speaking with the power of a proclamation from on high, she gave the quantity Aaron had confided in her.

The man nearly choked. The look in his eyes grew stronger, all but dilating with greed.

She had him.

If he could sell even a fraction of the gold Flora's mines produced, for even a small percentage, he would become one of the wealthiest men in the region. And he knew it.

One of the elders was saying something about taxes and the benefit to the city. Azeda ignored him.

"Why me?" he asked. "Others could do what you ask. You could do it yourself."

"Few are as ruthless as you," Rechab answered. "I would rather not be in competition with an operation as efficient and large in scale as yours. Partnership suits me much better."

Even without Flora's experience, Rechab knew what that sort of competition looked like—as much a matter of swords and assassins as it was of prices and trusts. She hoped she might actually be speaking some truth on Flora's part.

Azeda was nodding now, rubbing his hands—hardly listening to her anymore. She knew his mind was running numbers, calculating the wealth he could already taste and feel. But he had to know a catch was coming. Even a woman as devout and otherworldly as Flora the Unlucky would surely have an angle.

Rechab knew she had her fish in the net, so she pressed her advantage.

     Rachel Starr Thomson

"There are stipulations, of course," she said.

"Of course," the man echoed, though his voice stiffened.

Rechab leaned forward. "Business must be conducted under the laws of the Great God. That is my way throughout the Sacred Land."

"I know this to be true," Azeda said, and the elders nodded.

"There must be a blessing said over the mines," Rechab continued, "and prayer said each morning."

The men were still nodding. All was a matter of course. The People still did many of these things as a matter of course, of national pride.

But now it was time to draw the line.

"You have slaves who are past the time of release. You must loose them, and you must allow parents to buy their children back for fair price. You must raise the wages of your workers and allow them fair access to judgment in the gates—judgment which must be carried out fairly."

Azeda sat back as though someone had shoved him. She kept her eyes on him. The old man who had initially greeted them said, "Of course we follow the traditional ways of the People. Some of the laws have fallen out of use . . ."

"They have not fallen out of *my* use," Rechab said, doing her best to take on Flora's haughty confidence. "I have not found them a burden to practice. I can deal with you in no other way."

"My apologies," Azeda said, "but you speak veiled accusations, and you have nothing to accuse us of. The elders you see before you enforce justice in accordance with the Great God's law."

They were all nodding. Rechab knew it was assert herself now or lose everything.

"I have reason to believe the contrary," she said. "I hear of wrongs not righted and injuries given no redress. I hear of children unjustly enslaved and of bribes received among the elders. I hear of mines allowed to maim and kill without repairs or reformation being made. I believe what I hear. Unless these things are changed, I can have no dealings with you."

They sputtered. She closed her eyes for a second and let them process her words. She knew what she had just done—but she also knew how badly they wanted her gold.

Flora's gold.

She forged on. "Of course, I will appoint my servants to see to it that these reforms are carried out."

"You are asking for a great deal of interference," Azeda said.

"I am asking for permission to bless you with abundance you cannot possibly create on your own," Rechab countered. "And in return only that you manage your affairs with justice. Is that so high a price to pay?"

Azeda stood. The deep trouble of his expression was clear—this was a man in whom power and greed wrestled, for he saw himself needing to give up one in order to gain the other.

Rechab's mind was struck by a thousand ways this could go wrong, and she trembled. She hoped they could not see the trembling. Aaron's presence beside her, golden and strong, comforted her.

The big man turned his back on her and faced the elders. His voice boomed out. "Gold. It would do great things for us."

"For you especially, Azeda," the oldest man countered. "Is the blessing to us worth the loss of our freedom to manage as we see fit? To turn the rule of elders over to strangers?"

"You said it yourself," Azeda argued. "Gold would benefit us all."

"I do not like the thought of having her servants reigning over

     Rachel Starr Thomson

us," one of the other elders said. "Why should strangers judge our decisions?"

"We are free men," another said. "She asks us to become little more than slaves ourselves."

"But the benefits are great," Azeda insisted.

Rechab had been holding her breath, but at this point she began to feel angry. Their indignation was as much as a confession that they had been unjust in their treatment of their people. They had not said one word to argue with her accusations—not a single sentence to protest their innocence with facts or justify themselves. They argued only to preserve their liberty to continue trampling the liberty of others.

Kol Abaddon's prophecies and accusations burned through her mind. No wonder the Great God was angry with the People.

It was not lost on her that before she had claimed Flora's name, she had nearly been enslaved by this same kind of injustice, and there would have been no one to speak for her or rescue her.

No one to do what she was trying to do.

Righteous indignation and satisfaction flared within her, side by side. Aaron had been right to push her to do this. It was indeed what Flora would do. No matter how wrong things could go, it was evil that men like this should continue to mistreat their own countrymen simply because they could.

She stood. All eyes fixed on her in surprise.

"I have no need to listen to your debating," she said. "I will leave my servant with you to hear your conclusion. The choice is simple. You may act as you ought—in justice and in compliance with the Great God's laws. And if you do, you will be blessed with greater abundance than you know. Or you may impoverish yourselves in every respect by choosing to maintain the corruption of your ways."

And then she added, "But if you choose the latter, I warn you that not only will blessing not come to you, but retribution will."

She turned on her heel and stalked away, flushed with anger and beginning to shake at her own daring. Where had that come from?

Voices rose behind her. Aaron would be her ears—listening not only for their conclusion but for threats. Two of Flora's retinue, armed and imposing men, came forth to greet her and walk on either side of her. Their eyes questioned, but they asked nothing, and she said nothing. Just kept her head up and walked away, shaken and burning with anger.

Aaron caught up with her, flushed with elation, before she had made it back to Flora's tents. "They'll do it! They've agreed to convene a grievance hearing tomorrow, under our personal supervision. We may send our men to oversee changes at the mines. You've done it, Rechab! There will be justice for these people!"

Her own cheeks flushed. She wanted to laugh and cry at the same time.

But she didn't understand.

"How—why—"

"They could see you meant business. Storming away like that was a stroke of brilliance."

"I don't think it was me, Aaron—surely you deserve the credit as much as I do."

His eyes smiled as broadly as his mouth. "No, no . . . this victory belongs to Flora Laurentii. And to her beautiful deputy."

Now her blush deepened farther, and he cleared his throat and reddened for a new reason.

"They will be alerting the people of the hearing even tonight. They will bring their needs to the elders and justice will be done. Because of you, Rechab. Because of you."

RACHEL STARR THOMSON

Aurelius sat at the king's table amid a crowd of nobles and court-iers, all awaiting the arrival of their monarch. Shem, a young servant who had grown up in Aurelius's household, stood the requisite four feet behind his master, hands respectfully behind his back, awaiting any need or request.

Aurelius helped himself to the platters of grapes, figs, and apricots laid out before them and worked to ignore his irritation with his servant. He'd caught Shem donning an amulet of Amon-Heth that morning, and though he had never really inquired as to his servants' spiritual affinities before, he found himself unaccountably irked.

To add to that, Shem had been surly and distracted lately—ever since he'd returned from trying to track down Rechab in the desert. As urgent as everything felt in light of the killings in Nadab's household, Aurelius couldn't abide anyone near him being less than attentive. It made him feel as though a part of himself was dangerously scattered.

Marah, thank the Great God, understood. She remained sharp and focused. At this moment she dined with the king's second wife, though the invitation had not been easy to procure. The death of Beniah's favor-ite had dampened life in the palace in a way neither of the other wives had managed to lift, and they were not at the peak of their hospitality.

Raucous laughter from the cluster of young princes at one end of the long table overpowered the hushed talk of older men closer to Aurelius. None had engaged him in conversation, a circumstance he knew he should rectify if he was to make the most of his time in Shalem. He had not come all the way here to play the recluse.

But it was Beniah he truly wanted to converse with. In less than a day he had already seen the influence of Kimash overshadowing Shalem to an alarming degree. If he was to challenge the cult's encroachment on Bethabara and their murder of Nadab's household, he would need a powerful ally.

So instead of striking up conversation with any of the men at the table, Aurelius listened.

It took effort to train his ears to the murmurs beneath the laughter and loud clamor of the younger men, who were already deep in their wine cups and seemed insensate to the mourning that should still be affecting those closest to the king.

With surprise he heard one of the old men scorning the young drunks as "just as bad as the king."

Surely the king was not celebrating. Perhaps the elder meant that Beniah had been drowning his grief in too much wine.

Aurelius grimaced wryly. That was not an admirable trait for a king, but it was one a Westlander could hardly fault.

Conversations and drunken laughter hushed alike as fanfare announced the king's arrival, preceded by a wave of richly dressed servants and attendees with banners and palm fans. Aurelius searched through the faces for Beniah.

He was not prepared for what he saw.

The king seemed to have dropped ten years off his age. His face shone, well oiled; his eyes sparkled. He was laughing.

Aurelius's glimpse of him in the temple had not revealed this change. But as Beniah took his place at the head of the table, greeted with raised cups and cheers by the young rabble rousers, Helchi's words came whisking back:

Marriage, my friend. Marriage.

As the king sat on the cushions at the head of the table, acknowl-

 Rachel Starr Thomson

edging the greetings good-naturedly, Aurelius did not even have to listen to the returning buzz of conversation to know what Helchi had meant. Kimash was on the rise because of marriage—the *king's* marriage.

Beniah was taking another wife to replace the one he had lost. And in some way she was tied to the god of the Hill People.

Voices behind him made him aware that Shem was talking to the other servants.

"Shem!" he snapped.

"Sir?" the servant asked, stepping forward immediately.

"Attend me. Stay out of this idle chatter."

"Sir?"

His order was out of character, and he knew it. Conversation with the palace servants might even benefit him, if Shem could learn news or gossip and relay it later. But he didn't want the boy talking. Or listening. Or having anything to do with whatever was happening in this city.

He didn't want to explain himself, so instead he said shortly, "Fetch me new wine."

Shem hesitated a moment, perhaps to point out that Aurelius had not taken more than a drop of the wine in front of him now, but he thought better of it and obediently went to seek out his master's request.

"You seem out of sorts, friend," a white-bearded man on Aurelius's left said.

"It was a long journey here," Aurelius answered.

The old man raised an eyebrow. His blue robes bespoke great wealth, and Aurelius thought he looked familiar.

"From Bethabara? Hardly more than a day's journey up the mountain. But you have not attended here for some time, Florus Laurentinus."

Aurelius shook his head. "Would you believe Shalem feels farther away than it ever has?"

"You are disturbed by the king's newfound joy," the old man said, his voice low but clear. He took a sip of wine from a golden cup. "And by the presence of Kimash. I saw you staring at the high priest in the temple yesterday. Heed an old man's advice: veil your stares. He is a powerful man, and his influence here only grows."

Aurelius turned his head slowly until he looked at the man dead-on. Yes—he did know this face. Brown, weathered skin spoke of a life lived mainly outside the palace. The man's hands were large and deep-lined with age. Brown eyes sparkled with insight and equally with wisdom. Aurelius felt placated: this was a face that embodied the essence of the Holy People he had known all his life—a face that belonged here.

"I know your face," Aurelius said. "But your name escapes me, friend."

"I am called Ezra, son of Malchi. My father's fathers were princes of the desert slopes, and I follow in their footsteps."

"An auspicious history for one who sits so far from the king."

Ezra waved his brown hand dismissively at the far end of the table. "As you can see, the king prefers the company of fools."

Aurelius marveled at his boldness of speech, yet Ezra moderated his voice so well, and the distractions around the king's table were so many, that he doubted anyone else overheard.

"I have seen you many a time in court when I came here to treat for matters of judgment and care of my lands," Ezra said, "but in those days I was always only passing through. My sons had not yet taken on their princely duties and relieved me of mine. Many of the princes of the old families resented your position as governor."

"And you?" Aurelius asked.

    Rachel Starr Thomson

Ezra smiled, but it was a smile Aurelius couldn't completely read.

"You seemed to me a fine man and still do. I did not like the presence of strangers in the king's house. But now it seems the house is overrun with strangers."

He took a long, slow drink from his wine cup, and his brown eyes fixed on the far end of the table.

Beniah was rising from his pile of cushions to speak.

"My friends!" he said. His voice slurred slightly, to the palpable disapproval of the prince sitting next to Aurelius. "Celebrate with me today!"

A cheer went up, headed and carried by the young men but taken up by most around the table. Aurelius found he could not lift his voice, so he merely nodded his head in acknowledgment. He did not look at the man next to him, but he noted Ezra's stony silence.

Beniah raised his hands to quiet the crowd, but as he did, Aurelius caught sight of men stirring in the shadows of the far end of the room behind him. His blood ran cold.

They wore black, and among them he recognized the unmistakable form of Kimash's high priest.

And there was someone else . . .

"I call on you all to rejoice with me," Beniah continued, "for the gods have smiled on my broken heart and on our kingdom. I am soon to wed!"

He held up his hands again to dampen the cheers that rose at his announcement, louder this time, though Ezra remained silent and Aurelius found he too could not join in.

Shem bent over and set a new wine cup beside him, silent. Aurelius reached up and grabbed the young man's arm.

"Stay close," he hissed.

"In a mere fortnight I will seal our alliance with the Hill People and their god, Kimash, in my marriage to the most beautiful woman in the world."

Chuckles and laughter met his announcement along with more shouts of approval, and Beniah's face flushed red—with what emotion, Aurelius could not quite tell. He could not keep his eyes on the king. They continually strayed into the shadows, straining, trying to make out just who stood there and why their presence unnerved him so greatly.

And then Beniah half-turned, held out his hand, and announced, "That you might all rejoice with me properly, I have brought her here!"

This time the gathering erupted. With cheers, with ribald catcalls from the drunkest of the men, with protests. Ezra ben Malchi let out a cry of derision that was lost in the clamor of voices. For a woman to attend the king's table was not proper. Not decent, and not done.

Aurelius found himself involuntarily voicing something, but the sound died in his throat.

Out from the shadows, a woman stepped, her hand resting lightly on that of the high priest. The voices quieted as they came forward, the priest ushering her to the king and transferring her hand to his.

"I give you Izevel," Beniah beamed, "the future queen of the Sacred Land."

Dressed from head to foot in dark blue, her large green eyes outlined with kohl and her lips bright red in an ivory face, Izevel might in truth hold claim to be the most beautiful woman in the world. She walked tall, head high and haughty, a woman of stature who exuded a powerful, almost feral grace.

Shem gasped, but it was Aurelius who said aloud, barely realizing the words had escaped him, "She looks like Flora."

Thick dark hair cascaded down her back. Green eyes swept the table, bold, daring the men to challenge her even as she invited them to drink her in. She did, indeed, look like Flora.

Like Flora's dark angel, Aurelius thought.

Something in the woman's spirit was cold, almost cruel. She had none of Flora's fire.

The king panted at her side like a puppy. Even the high priest of Kimash paled in her presence. Ezra bristled but said not one word.

One thing was instantly clear to Aurelius.

With this woman at the king's side, Aurelius would find no help from Beniah against the murderous forces of Kimash.

CHAPTER 8

Rechab arrived for the judgment at the gates of Nachush the next morning in proper pomp, with all the ceremony and glamor Aaron knew to enact. He helped her off her white mule with a strong hand and whispered in her ear, "Be strong and glory in this day. You are doing a marvelous thing."

With a smile at him that she hoped didn't look too nervous, she turned to greet and be greeted by the elders. The group of seven men looked various shades of unhappy to see her. Azeda alone did not seem bothered—if anything, his expression was smug.

Rechab seated herself on a high rock. Aaron stood behind her with his hands clasped behind his back.

"Let the court of the city open!" Azeda boomed. A crier took up the call, and it echoed through the street . . .

The *empty* street.

Troubled, Rechab swept the streets with her eyes for some sign of the supplicants she and Aaron had come to help. From what the beggars had told her, there should be dozens of them. Azeda had sent out messages the night before, alerting all the city to the opportunity to bring their grievances to a fair trial, held under the Great God's laws.

That Rechab was not *exactly* sure what those laws entailed troubled her somewhat, but Aaron had assured her that he knew enough to make sure justice was done for the people. She did know some herself. Restitution was to be made, in payment or vengeance, for bodily harm done by another. Slaves were not to be held past the terms determined by their debts—or their parents' debts. Money that had been stolen through fraud had to be returned in double or triple measure.

All of these crimes, the beggars had assured her and Aaron, stained Azeda's hands. Every man and woman in the city could make a case against him. The messages that went out the night before had promised he would pay. The judgment against him would fall so hard that he would be removed from his position, and the elders, now bound to Rechab through the agreement they had all made, would be forced to see it done.

Yet no one was here.

Rechab licked her lips and looked behind her at Aaron, who sternly motioned for her to look forward again. She should not look too dependent on him—Flora Laurentii, after all, was famous for her confidence.

"It is early," he whispered.

Azeda and the other elders began to whisper among themselves, and then to talk and laugh out loud. Their conversation revolved around the mines, profits, local gossip. They did not seem concerned that anyone would come with a grievance.

Around noon—three hours after Rechab had arrived—a lone man limped into the wide open space before the gates. She sat up straighter, her heart leaping—with fear or with joy, she did not know. The elders, too, ceased their talk and bored into the man with their gazes. She could feel the tension in Aaron from behind her, though she did not turn back to look.

 RACHEL STARR THOMSON

"Judgment is in session," one of the elders intoned as the man drew near. "Have you a grievance to bring before this council?"

"Indeed," the man said. His voice shook. In looks he was no different from anyone else in the town—thin, with a hungry look in his eyes, his clothes threadbare and worn.

"Let us hear it," Azeda boomed.

The man trembled even harder, and to Rechab's surprise, he got down on his knees in the dust. She was about to protest, but Aaron's light touch on her back stopped her.

"Please, Azeda," the man said, "you remember me. I came to your house only two nights ago."

"You did," Azeda boomed. "You sold me a rug."

"I did," the man said, still on his knees in the dirt. With a jerky, sudden motion, he reached into his shirt and pulled out a battered coin.

"Please, my lord," he said. "I did not tell you the truth about its age—it is older than I said. I fear I overcharged you."

Rechab found that she could not breathe. A grin slowly spread across Azeda's face.

The man stammered, "I charged you a half-shekel more than I should have."

"You stole from me, then," Azeda said.

"Y-yes, my lord." The man held out the coin in his shaking hand. "But I have brought t-twice the amount in restitution."

Azeda motioned for one of his servants to retrieve the coin. The servant did, pausing to look censoriously down on the man who still remained on his knees in the dirt.

Azeda received the coin, examined it by holding it up before his face and turning it around once or twice, and then pocketed it with a satisfied smile. "You may go," he told the man. "I will press no further charges against you."

"Thank you—thank you," the man said. He got up and ran off, leaving the marks of his presence in the dust.

Rechab's mind was spinning. This—Azeda's vindication! This was not what she had come here to see. This was not why she had gone so far in this charade, offering Flora's gold and joining hands with these devils. She and Aaron had intended to bring these men to justice, not enrich them still further!

Aaron bent down, and she heard his voice in her ear. He was carefully controlling it—trying to hide his anger and worry.

"We have only passed the morning," he said. "The people are busy in their homes. As the day goes on, they will come."

But the day went on, and though the sun rose higher and the town and the mines stirred with life, the people did not come.

It took Aurelius two more days to secure a private audience with the king. Marah encouraged him to be patient, but she too seemed antsy about the delay. Izevel's arrival had upset the balance of life in the Holy City, sweeping the whole of the court and most of the commoners too up in a whirl of feasting, festivities, and drunken revelry. And, disturbingly, public sacrifices and demonstrations of worship to Kimash.

If the god of the Hill People had been sickening the city from under the surface, now he broke out like a pox on its very skin: every street corner and alley became an altar to the two-headed deity of the hills.

          RACHEL STARR THOMSON

Aurelius made his way to the palace with the edge of his blue mantle held over his nose. The air was full of smoke and incense and the smell of wine and blood. Laughter and shrieks, just the tip of the general pandemonium, echoed in the narrow streets.

Aurelius's guards followed a few paces behind him, eyes sharp for trouble. The governor of Bethabara found within himself a growing loathing for what was happening all around him. His forefathers had been as debauched as the next wealthy man, but they at least had kept their revelry to the appropriate times and places. The public streets, only weeks after the last queen's death, were neither.

Nor did he understand or sympathize with the worshippers. Aurelius was not a religious man: he believed in the spiritual world, of course, but viewed it with a cynical eye. Religion was politics, for the most part, just like everything else. The kind of wild, unfettered "devotion" displayed by the infatuated followers of Kimash was disgusting and strange to him.

He hoped that the king was not personally swayed by it, no matter what his new bride's ancestral religion was. He did not really fear that Beniah *would* be—the only religion he actually owed anything to was that of the Great God, and he had never been particularly devoted there. There was little reason to believe he would suddenly become an ardent worshipper of some foreign spirit.

Nodding to the palace guards who opened for him, Aurelius passed out of the chaotic streets and into the quieter, more dignified halls of the king's home. He dropped the corner of his mantle and breathed easier here. Laughter echoed from distant rooms here too, but it was the laughter of the gentlefolk before they've had opportunity to become too drunk, not the unrestrained shrieks of the common people.

A steward greeted Aurelius and ushered him to a spacious anteroom where the king sat on a low wicker throne, fanned by a slave and eating from a bowl of grapes.

"My lord!" Aurelius said, forcing himself to sound heartier than he felt. "My congratulations on your upcoming marriage."

"Thank you, thank you my friend," Beniah beamed. "Have you seen her? Of course you have . . . you were there two nights ago, I remember. When I introduced her to the men of the court."

Breaking about two centuries' worth of protocol and propriety, Aurelius did not add. Instead he said, "She's very beautiful, your majesty."

"And you're very glib," Beniah said. "Always the politician with the gilded tongue. You've been wanting an audience with me for days, I think. I apologize for keeping you waiting. I have been terribly busy."

The king, of course, owed him no apology, but Beniah had always been humble in that way. It was one reason the court liked him and generally did not oppose him, even covertly. Beniah was often manipulated, but he did not have enemies.

"I understand this is a busy time," Aurelius said. "Full of demands on you."

"And yet you come with another," Beniah said with a grin. "Well, out with it. What did you want to see me about?"

Aurelius was unable to keep the grimace from his face.

Beniah's grin faded. "Oh . . . it's something serious, is it?"

"I fear so. In fact, your majesty, it's both serious and urgent. There's been an attack in Bethabara that must be dealt with, and I believe you must be seen to be the one dealing with it."

"An attack? What are you talking about? Some bandit strike—or don't tell me, Kol Abaddon's armies have arrived at last!"

Beniah burst out laughing at that, and Aurelius fought to keep anger from reddening his cheeks. This was no time for mockery.

     Rachel Starr Thomson

"Someone ordered the murder of an entire household," he said, keeping his voice tightly controlled. "The household of Nadab the Trader—you know him; he's a wealthy merchantman, a man of no small influence. Nadab himself was left alive, but all but one of his servants were slaughtered. I tried to keep it hushed up, but by now word will have spread through the town. I have been here some days waiting for an audience with you, as you yourself have already acknowledged."

Beniah looked aghast at him. "Murdered a household! What . . . five people, six—"

"Twenty-two," Aurelius said. Any attempt at humor and goodwill failed him as the grim facts of the situation came to the fore. "Nadab is a man of means."

Beniah said nothing. Aurelius pressed his point once more. "Bethabara is not a large town. The deaths are significant, and they will cause panic. This will come down on my head. As governor, the people will hold me responsible. That is why I am here. As your representative in Bethabara, I ask you to send your own forces to bring swift retribution."

"Of course," Beniah said. His ruddy face had gone pale. "Of course, Aurelius. You have a right to expect that. The *people* have a right to expect that."

A ground swell of relief swept through Aurelius, and he sighed, feeling momentarily unsteady on his feet. He bowed his head. "I thank you, my lord. You are quick to grasp the situation."

"We must investigate," Beniah said. "Find out who is responsible."

"Unnecessary," Aurelius said. "We already know that. I can provide you with eyewitnesses if you need them to confirm the facts, but I have investigated already and can tell you exactly who is responsible."

At this news Beniah sat up straighter and slapped his knee. "Well? Out with it!"

"The work was done by assassins who work for the high priest of Kimash."

At Beniah's instant change of expression—from eager and angry to bewildered—Aurelius hastened to add, "Of course, you need not implicate the high priest himself. We can keep that much hidden from the people. All that needs to be done is the murderers themselves brought to justice. That will calm the people's fears and restore their faith in you and in me to protect them and keep a handle on what's happening in this kingdom."

But the color had not returned to Beniah's face.

"I don't know . . ." he said slowly.

Aurelius had to remind himself that this was the king, and it was not acceptable or wise to lose his temper. So instead, he said, "I don't understand. This was a crime—a blatant and bloody one. I have all the proof necessary to prosecute the culprits."

But Beniah was shaking his head. "My wife," he said, "that is, my bride . . . the high priest . . ."

The incoherent babble turned Aurelius's face a shade hotter, but he kept his composure and waited for Beniah to form a sentence.

"I cannot act too rashly against my allies," Beniah finally said. He moved as though to pick up a chalice of wine, but there wasn't one to hand.

"Respectfully, my lord, in this instance your allies have moved against you. Surely you cannot just ignore that?"

"No, no," Beniah said. "I will speak with the high priest."

Aurelius's face twitched. He wanted very much to protest, but it wasn't as though Beniah could bring the killers to justice without the high priest's knowledge—so perhaps it would not hurt to bring the man in now.

  RACHEL STARR THOMSON

"Will you do so quickly?" Aurelius asked. "I have been away too long already. At a time like this I do not think it wise to let matters fester in the town."

"Of course," Beniah said, sounding a little more assured of himself again. "Are you staying in your estate outside the city?"

"Yes, with Marah."

"I will send you word within two more nights. As soon as I can, Aurelius, I promise."

It was too long—Aurelius would rather have had an answer that same night—but all he could realistically hope for. He nodded unhappily. Bethabara would just have to wait a little longer.

⸻◆⸻

When he arrived in the courtyard of his estate, the sun had set just far enough below the horizon to cast a pall of deep blue over the Holy Mountain and the valleys below it. Aurelius paused to look out over the view, torches blazing behind him on the porch of his house to welcome him home. He could see the flickering lights of Bethabara, down a winding road halfway down the mountain—the last town before one reached the Holy City. No word had come of a crisis breaking out there; he hoped that meant things were still under control.

People, his grandfather and father had taught him, need only three things to remain peacefully subservient: safety, food, and the sense that justice is not out of their reach. Take one of those three away, and discontent will breed like rats; and like rats, discontent in the end will bring disaster. Most especially on the man of the house.

Thanks to the high priest's murderous intrusion, two of the three had been stolen. The people of Bethabara could not feel safe, and if the deaths of so many innocent were not quickly avenged, they would begin to feel themselves victims of injustice.

Well, Aurelius was doing the best he could. He could not speed up the process.

He walked inside. "Marah! Shem!"

His wife appeared in the open corridor within moments. His servant did not.

"You're in a foul mood," Marah observed.

Aurelius sighed. "Looks are deceiving. Not foul, just impatient. The king will move, but he fears upsetting the high priest of Kimash, so he will not move until he has talked to him."

"Given the new connections at court, that should not surprise us."

He sighed again. "I suppose it doesn't. But it frustrates me nonetheless. The people have already waited so long."

"Word has come from Bethabara that Nadab is gone," Marah said. "He left with his only remaining servant several days ago. Seeking his daughter, rumor says."

Aurelius only nodded. That was not a great surprise, though it meant his promised eyewitnesses would not be at hand if Beniah needed them. He looked around. "Where is Shem?"

Marah hesitated, to her husband's surprise. "He asked leave of me to attend celebrations in the city," she said. "I gave it to him."

"You what?" Aurelius snapped. "Why? I want him here."

"He has seemed strained since he returned from the desert. Overworked, perhaps—or just bothered by the same thing that bothers you."

"*He* does not have the weight of an entire town's trust on his shoulders."

     Rachel Starr Thomson

"But he has the weight of yours, and you have been hard on him lately."

Aurelius shot Marah a pointed look. Shem had been raised in their house. He was the age their son would have been had the child survived, and Marah had always been fond of him—too fond, in Aurelius's opinion.

"It's only one night," Marah said. "I hoped it would lighten his spirits."

"What is happening out there," Aurelius said, punctuating the last two words with a jab of his finger over his shoulder, "is more likely to hang a man's spirit over for days."

"Shem is a good boy," Marah said. "So he may get a little drunk. He'll be better for it after a day or two."

Aurelius gave a momentary thought to getting a little drunk himself. But he remembered the king's flushed face and the rioting revelers in the streets and thought better of it.

⸻ ◆ ⸻

In the shadows of an alley dancing with oil light, Shem crept through the crowds with furtive glances to his right and left. His hand rested near his neck, cradling the amulet of Amon-Heth.

"Come here, boy!" a painted woman called from a doorway. From the lit house behind her laughter pealed through the air, and revelers crammed the space so tightly they seemed as though they would burst out through the walls. "Come in and feast with us!"

Shem ignored her, shouldering his way through tightly packed groups of partiers. Never in his life had he seen such a celebration, such a crowded, noisy, chaotic expression of excess. Not in Bethabara—where there were not enough people to pack the streets like this no matter what the occasion—and not even here, in Shalem, on the many prior visits with Aurelius and Marah.

He had told Marah he wanted to go and see the party, to partake in the feasting and the delight of the crowds. The coming of the new queen had opened the way for unrestrained merriment after the subdued hush of the last queen's death. And because the Hill People were themselves so known for excess and for chaos, and because the god of the Hill People had undeniably become a celebrity in the past several weeks, the current climate of the city allowed for a celebration the likes of which the Holy People might never before have felt freedom to hold.

Yes, Shem had told Marah he wanted to come and partake in it all. But the truth was that all this scared and troubled him. When the woman called to him from the doorway he felt a thrill, yes; his surroundings thrilled him in beckoning, sensual ways, but even his own reaction to it made him want to crawl down a hole and hide. He felt like a little boy trying to navigate his way through a world that was far too adult, where it seemed violence and thievery might lurk around every corner—ready to steal his very soul.

He finally made his way through the city to the narrow street where the summons had told him to go. This street was quieter—a drunk had collapsed at the head of it, but it was barely wide enough for a man to slip through, and no lamps lit its shadows. He wedged himself past the drunk, up the narrow way between whitewashed walls, and paused in front of a tall door, shut fast.

Dim light slipping out the cracks of the door indicated that yes, someone was at home. He looked again at the note in his hand telling him where to go. Yes, this should be the place.

Taking a deep breath, he knocked.

 RACHEL STARR THOMSON

As the sounds of the party drifted through the air, he waited what seemed a very, very long minute. Then the door opened, and a voice—he could not see whose voice it was—said, "Enter."

He slipped inside, and the door closed behind him. The house was close and narrow like the street, and nearly as dark. A shadowy servant slipped away from behind him, saying "Wait here."

Shem did, nervously shifting from foot to foot. The dim light came from another room just off this one, partially blocked with a curtain. In the shadows he could see little about this place, but it seemed to him bare—not from poverty but from a clean, polished asceticism. A smell he did not recognize tinged the air, sharp. Some sort of ointment, perhaps.

The servant—a small man, slightly bent at the shoulders, pulled the curtain aside suddenly and said, "Come."

Shem nodded and nervously entered the room beyond.

His host, a tall man with a shaved head and darkly painted eyes, looked up at him. He sat on a low, ornate stool. It was the only piece of furniture in the room. A single oil lamp burned on the floor in one corner.

The Southerner wore only a short kilt—and around his neck, an amulet like Shem's. A figure of Amon-Heth. His skin glistened with the ointment that tinged the air.

The man did not smile or acknowledge Shem except with the slightest nod, but Shem felt . . . better in his presence.

"You had a safe journey?" Shem asked.

A slight nod again.

"This is an unusual time in the city."

The man spoke. "It is disgusting."

Shem felt that he agreed. Certainly, he far preferred the company of this stranger and the way he kept his house—clean, disciplined, controlled.

Shem cleared his throat and waited, having run very quickly out of polite things to say.

The man finally said something on his own. "You have the reports my master wants?"

Shem tried not to let his sigh of relief be heard. "I do. I have done just as he told me—kept my eyes and ears open to everything. I have been in the very courts of the king. Amon should be pleased that . . ."

"Amon will be pleased if he wishes to be pleased. Give me your messages and I will pass them on."

Shem nodded.

He proceeded to report everything he knew. The assassins' attacks in Bethabara and the connection to the high priest of Kimash. The presence of that very high priest both in the temple and in the palace of the Holy City. His connection to the king's new bride, Izevel, and the way the whole city now seemed to dance in Kimash's shadow. He held nothing back, although his conscience twinged when he related some detail that he thought Aurelius would rather have kept to himself.

After all, it was only information, and it was all true. There could be no harm in spreading truth—and Amon was paying well.

Most significantly of all, Amon-Heth had led Shem into this relationship himself—or itself, as might be more appropriate. Had he not seen an apparition of the Southern god pointing him to Amon's camp while he was supposed to be searching for Nadab's daughter Rechab? Amon-Heth had appeared to him.

That was better than he could say for Kimash, and ten thousand times better than anyone could say for the Great God.

     RACHEL STARR THOMSON

The man—a high-ranking servant of Amon the Southern Trader—listened carefully. Shem knew he would repeat every word exactly as it had been recited, just as Shem had been careful to remember every detail exactly as it had transpired. He hoped the servant noticed what a skilled reciter he was: Marah had allowed him some schooling as a child, and he knew he was gifted in this area. He was grateful.

Finally he finished, and uncertain what he should do next, he shuffled from one foot to another again.

The servant looked slightly annoyed. He held out his closed fist in Shem's direction and then, without a word, opened it.

A large coin sat in the palm of his hand. Shem reached out hesitantly, and the servant waited until he had taken it before drawing his hand back. He turned his shaved head slightly in the direction of the street. Noise was growing closer.

"Kimash," the man said, but somehow he drew the word out so that it dripped with disdain.

Shem turned to go. At the door, he paused and turned back. He had almost forgotten.

"There is one more thing," he said. "But I do not know what it means or if Amon . . ."

"Tell me," the man said.

Shem nodded and swallowed. "Izevel . . . the king's new bride. She looks like Flora Laurentii."

When the man did not react, Shem said, "She could be her sister. Even a twin."

The man nodded.

As Shem made his way back out of the city, toward the hillside where the wealthy estates protected themselves from the commoners with armed guards and expensive entertainments, the disdain for

Kimash that Amon's servant had voiced grew inside of him, protecting him against the revelers and the temptations they so openly flaunted.

Alongside it grew a conviction that Amon-Heth and the other gods of the South, with their great power and their terrifying discipline, were worthy of his esteem and even his worship.

Rachel Starr Thomson

CHAPTER 9

The night of the failed judgment, lying in Flora's tent with the moonlight dimly shining through the fabric above her, Rechab blinked away tears of anger and shame and wondered if she had imagined the three beggars who had pleaded with her to use Flora's power to make things right for them.

But of course she had not. They were real; their grievances were more than real. They were mirrored in man after man, woman after woman, family after family—all with their own stories, their own desperate needs, their own grievances. She could see them skulking in their houses and coming in and out of the mines. The bleeding need of this city for justice was evident to anyone with eyes.

But not one had come to the hearing.

Azeda had sat smug and triumphant while a tiny trickle of villagers came only to declare their fealty, their happiness with the way things were. One or two denounced the interference of outsiders. Azeda and his puppet elders had run these people with fear too long, and Flora's money, powerful though it was, was not enough to counter that after all.

Aaron, angry and almost frantic, had finally rushed away from the proceedings to the mines and the village to ensure Azeda had not done something to keep the people away. But he had not. The people were free to come.

And they chose to stay away.

"Why?" Rechab burst out, knowing there was no one here to hear her. Glad of that.

Except she wasn't glad. She was alone, and hurting, and hating it.

She wanted Alack.

With a start she realized she hadn't thought of Alack in weeks. Not since becoming Flora Laurentii, really. Guilt crept into her chest as she realized she'd let Aaron take his place. But what else was she supposed to do? She was a woman on the run. Alack was who-knew-where, apprenticed to the mad prophet. Theirs had been a childhood romance, and it was not here for her now.

But what to do about the people?

She knew they needed help. Azeda was killing them. Stealing from them. Enslaving them. Truly, the justice she and Aaron had offered only went halfway—true justice would no doubt see Azeda dead. A fragment of the ancient law of the Great God ran through her head, an oft-spoken relic of the past: *Eye for eye, tooth for tooth, life for life, blood for blood.*

She shuddered.

She could not sleep. Not like this.

Wrapping herself in a veil, Rechab rose and paced the tent, her feet following a rut in the ground that seemed made for midnight fretting. It was too deep for the rugs to hide; strange that her entourage had set up her tent here, on ground so deeply rutted.

Her retinue. *Her* tent. It was all a joke—all a waste. Flora had given her the world, and she wasn't capable of doing anything with it.

She wasn't sure why her feet took her out the door. What she

     RACHEL STARR THOMSON

intended to do. Who she thought she was to charge out into the moonlight and seek answers.

For a moment, in her wild state of mind, she thought she wanted to grab a knife and bring justice to Azeda by her own hand.

But no, of course she didn't want to do that. She calmed herself down with the thought.

So what was she doing out here?

The moon overhead was bright. Beyond it, stars danced their tangled dance. Told their stories. She wished she understood them. Any of them.

In Shalem, what seemed a world from here, some had taken to worshipping the stars. They believed that since the stars could tell the future to those who understood, they also controlled it.

That was nonsense, Rechab thought, staring up into the vastness of the sky.

She shivered.

It was cold out here.

Strange how a day blazing with heat could cool so far down in the darkness as to become a different place, threatening travelers with very different dangers. Die of heatstroke during the day. Freeze to death at night. And yet it was all one desert, one wilderness.

Her thoughts were still resisting her attempts to wrestle them under control, so she picked up her feet and started walking again. To her surprise, she found the same rut that ran under her tent. It continued along the ground, leading away from the camp toward the town.

She followed.

Deep in her mind, she could hear Alack warning her not to do this. A long time ago, when she was just a child, she had liked to wander at night. Sometimes she had done it awake; sometimes asleep. A sleepwalker, frightening her sisters. Alack took her to task for wandering away from her father's walled house, his boyish finger wagging sternly in her face.

"It is dangerous out of doors at night, Rechab," he had said. "There are jackals and hyenas and goat demons."

"There are none of those things in Bethabara," she had argued.

His frown only grew deeper. "In the town there are worse things than jackals. A bad man is worse than any beast."

She had admired him. He was so wise, even though he was just her age. Even though he smelled like sheep.

"How do you know all these things?" she asked.

"My father has told me," he said.

"And you believe all that your father tells you?"

Why had she asked that question? She paused in her following of the rutted path, thinking back. Yes, she had said those very words. He'd said yes, of course he did, and looked confused. And now she remembered: that was when she first knew that her father, Nadab the Trader, was not like Naam, the Shepherd. Because Naam could be trusted, and Nadab could not. Even then she knew that.

Even then she knew that money was the most important thing in her father's world, and that he would lie for it sometimes. Or at least hide things. Sometimes important things.

Like the reality of her impending marriage.

Like selling her to Kimash.

Her eyes filled with tears, and impatiently she wiped them away with the heel of her hand, standing still in the rut.

Life was too much. And her father was wrong—money couldn't

fix things. She knew that now. Because she had all the money anyone could wish for, and it had fixed nothing.

Maybe that was why Flora had run off to Essea—the desert community with its austere lifestyle and its studies and prayers. All the more usual answers to life's questions had turned up empty.

When she got enough control over herself to stop her sobs and clear away her tears, lights twinkled before her. Nachush.

A sudden, crazy resolution gripped her.

Ignoring Alack's long-ago warnings and her own good sense, she brushed herself off, wrapped her veil more tightly around herself, and descended into the town.

Rechab wandered down narrow streets shrouded in shadow. The few lights that flickered shone from oil lamps in windows. The lights reminded her that even though she was angry with these people for refusing to seek their own good when they had a chance, they were good people. Decent people. Lights in a window meant welcome to strangers in need.

Well, she was a stranger. And in her own way, she was in great need.

She ascended the steps of a small, nondescript house wedged in among others and lifted her hand to knock. Hesitated. She was mad, surely. More kinds of a fool than her sisters had ever called her for walking at night.

A fool born then, she decided, and breeding had done nothing for it.

She knocked.

After an agonizingly long moment during which Rechab's heart raced and she nearly turned and ran, the door cracked open and someone peered out at her.

The eyes that looked out were both curious and fearful at first, but a moment later the expression turned to confusion, and then something she didn't expect—disgust. The door would have slammed in her face had she not reached out and caught it, preventing the owner from closing it all the way.

"Be off," the woman on the other side said. "We don't want your kind here."

It took Rechab a moment to realize she was being taken for a prostitute—the only kind of young woman likely to be out alone at night.

"No, you are mistaken," she said. "I am not . . . what you think. Please, let me in."

The door opened almost immediately, revealing a woman of middle age. Her inquisitive stare was intrusive and not exactly friendly, but she swung the door open and indicated that Rechab should enter.

"Who are you, then? And what do you need?"

"Just shelter," Rechab said, entering while she could. She wasn't convinced the door wouldn't slam in her face again a moment later if she waited. "Shelter and company."

"Good you didn't say food," another voice said, this one from a dark corner of the house. "Seeing as we've got none."

Rechab picked her words carefully. "Are you victims of famine?" she asked.

The woman cackled. "Not famine, but the lack caused by hands too greedy and eyes yellow with bribes and blood."

Rechab closed her eyes a split second. "May I ask . . ." she paused, searching for words again. How to present herself? "I . . . heard . . . that the elders of the village invited all to come and seek justice today. Because of . . . of Flora Laurentii. And the Great God. Did you not take your needs to them?"

The man barked a laugh. "And expect justice from unjust men? Why?"

"Because . . . well, from what I heard, because the men are entering into partnership with Flora Laurentii, and she insists they change their ways."

Rechab cleared her throat, hoping her nerves came across as the reticence of a stranger to speak too freely or boldly in the presence of her hosts. "Flora is a powerful woman, they say."

"Flora the Unlucky," the man said. "That is what they call her all over the Sacred Land. She will bring only misfortune to the likes of us. Has she not already? We had one master, now we have two, and one so far away we can have no recourse to her. She's here now, but she'll leave in a few days, and then what? Then we are twice-bound and alone."

The woman nodded, her voice twisted with bitterness. "She may be a good-hearted stranger. All accounts say she is. But you can't buy goodness in no one. She's a fool if she thinks she can. All she brings us is slavery again. And perhaps, then, that's what she is really—just another slaver who pretends to be good."

Rechab nodded slowly. She sank to the floor, curling up against the wall as any other guest off the street might do when offered shelter.

Was that all she was?

A fool who was trying to bribe men into goodness?

Put that way, it did sound like an ill-hatched plan. And most likely ill-fated. All Aaron's passion set only to burn out and avail nothing.

"Then," she asked slowly, "what will you do? Will you stay here and starve?"

"What choice do we have?" the man asked bitterly. "Yes, we could leave. Become refugees in a land where strangers find few friends. Cross the wilderness in fear of bandits and jackals and demons. Find land we can farm—where? And who would give it to us? No, there's little choice for us."

He shifted, coming into the light and peering at Rechab. "You are a stranger yourself. A wanderer in our streets. You can't have come from far—one such as you would not survive the world as it is."

Rechab wanted to protest that that was not true, but she could hardly confess to the ruse. And anyway, telling her story would not prove her point. She had traveled a little on her own—from Essea to the bend of the river two days away. In that time she had nearly fallen victim to slavers and had been rescued only because she fell back on a name, wealth, and power that few refugees on the face of the earth could hope to claim.

The man was right. The Sacred Land was not a place where a woman could be safe on her own.

"I am a nomad," she lied. "My people passed through these parts several days ago, but I remained behind because I had fallen ill and needed rest. I am journeying to catch up with them now."

Even as the words came out, she kicked herself a thousand times over for all the holes in the story. These people would know nomads had not come through their valley. They would know better than to believe she had been left behind alone. She did not look like she had recently been ill—so ill that she could not remain with her people or they with her.

But her hosts did not ask.

The woman disappeared through a small door and a moment later came back holding a large piece of flat bread, which she tore. She handed Rechab a piece and gave another to her husband, who set to eating it in a surly manner despite his claims that they had no food.

Rechab did not want to accept the bread, but she realized she would be insulting her hosts if she did not. And besides that, she would make her story that much more unconvincing if she did not appear to be hungry. She ate, the bread tasting much like dust in her mouth, and cursed her own thoughtlessness.

But it was all right, she told herself. She would find a way to make a difference to these people, and soon they would have bread to spare. And more besides.

As she ate, her eyes darted around the little room. Its mud-daubed walls and earthen floor were plain and bare but for a pallet and a small table. A world away from the lavish life she had known in her father's house and in the tents of merchants all over the Sacred Land.

The woman disappeared through the small door again—little more than a rough opening in the wall, dark as a tomb on the other side—and emerged bearing a skin of wine and three clay cups. She poured the wine and handed it to Rechab and her husband, and again Rechab accepted despite her misgivings and tried to look appropriately eager to drink. She'd taken on this part, now she had no real choice but to play it.

She wanted to laugh at the thought that returning to her role as Flora Laurentii would feel like a return to reality. When had playing that part become so natural to her?

More natural, in some ways, than being Rechab the trader's daughter had ever been. Except, of course, when she was with Alack.

Thought of her friend troubled her and turned the bread and wine even more to dust in her mouth. She didn't know why. Perhaps because he was the one part of her old life she wished she could still have, but she was certain—more than certain—that her old life was gone forever. Gone, with its evils and its dreams alike.

Alack wouldn't approve of this, she thought suddenly.

But she didn't know why she thought that either.

"Flora Laurentii is a strange one to come here," the man of the house said suddenly. Rechab was so startled by the declaration that she nearly dropped the clay cup in her hand.

He went on. "Why here? Why now? Yes, the mines here are good. Rich. But not the best, and not the richest. Just rich enough to make our masters fat. Not enough to share with her, if you ask me. Rumor always said the woman knew trade, knew business. Knew mines. Now I start to doubt it."

"As though you know business," his wife chided.

"I know enough to call a bad deal bad," the husband retorted. "Don't you correct me, woman."

Rechab peered into her cup, the wine dark in the gloom of the little house. "Perhaps she has other reasons for coming here," she offered.

The man snorted. "No one does anything for any reason other than money."

Rechab's cheeks flushed. "That's not true. Some people do things because they care about others. Or because they believe in the Great God and want to obey him."

"Children do that, and fools," the man said. "Others say they do, but they're liars. Even Flora Laurentii. Mark you, she's a reason for being here that serves her own purposes, and it will make life none the better for us. You'll see."

He squinted across the room at Rechab. "You'll move on, I suppose, and find your family. Good. Keep on the move. It doesn't pay to be tied to the land—not anymore. In the old days the Great God blessed our inheritance, but now the whole land is cursed."

Rechab shuddered. For some reason the man's words reminded her of Kol Abaddon and his warnings of judgment.

The woman sniffed but said nothing. She eyed Rechab suspiciously,

     RACHEL STARR THOMSON

watching her drink—or avoid drinking, more like. "The Great God has forgotten us," she said flatly. "He has turned his eyes away and looks on some other people now. Better that we do as the nations and find a god who will turn his ear to us."

"It's not true," Rechab said before she really knew what she was saying.

The woman raised both eyebrows at her. "How's that?"

"It's not true that he has turned his eyes away," Rechab said, feeling her face flame. She was glad for the veil that hid her blush, though it could not hide the nervous passion in her voice. "He sees us. I have felt his eyes on me."

"Is that so?" the man asked. "Is that why you know so much about what drives Flora Laurentii to help us?"

This time Rechab's gratitude for the veil went even deeper—if they could see her face, she was sure it would give her away.

"If you should happen to be lying about yourself," the man said, "and if you should happen to have been sent here by Flora herself, or by one of her servants, to find out why we didn't come to the judgment in the gates today—well, if that should happen to be the case, you go back to your mistress and tell her that we did not come because we do not trust. Not her, not Azeda and the elders, not the Great God she claims to worship, and not the filthy lucre that is her real god."

"Shimon!" his wife said sharply.

Shimon glared at her. "I will speak my mind. The Great God does not hear us. I don't trust those who say they are his servants. He can't be moved, he can't be implored; we are better off worshipping gods who are like the elders—gods who will take bribes and do us favors when we ask."

"Like Kimash?" The words spilled out of Rechab's mouth before she could stop them.

"Yes, like Kimash," the man said, his eyes dark. "They say his star is ascendant. They say his influence grows even in the Holy City."

"I have seen that influence," Rechab shot back, shaking. "What it does to men. How it twists them and takes them over, as though they were animals."

He raised an eyebrow. "Then perhaps he will take over Azeda and remove him for us. Justice will be done here, girl. We don't need Flora Laurentii's help to do it."

"Husband!"

This time the shrill woman would not be denied. Shimon shrank back, sullen but visibly aware that he had said too much.

Rechab rose to go. She could not stay here longer—the man's words had rattled her too much. As she lifted her eyes, they fell on a niche in the wall—a crevice just higher than a man's head. And in it, a dark shape that she knew to be an idol. A torn piece of bread and a pile of figs sat on the shelf just in front of it, but she could make out its familiar two-headed outline.

"You worship your god," Shimon said calmly. "Leave us to worship ours."

 Rachel Starr Thomson

CHAPTER 10

When she decided that she could not abide under the idol's gaze a moment longer, Flora wasn't sure why she didn't go storming straight back to Amon to demand that the image of Kimash be torn down or else that she be moved. That would be the sensible thing to do, even though he was sure to argue with her and refuse to do as she wished, and she would have to demand and cajole and out-talk him until he gave in.

Instead she just charged out into the desert like a fool. The guards ran after her, growing closer and closer. She could almost hear their consternation as they tried to figure out what to do—grab her? Stop her? Ask her to come back? Assume she was running away and risk causing insult if they were wrong?

They were slaves, after all. Amon, with his gift of the scarlet dress and his courteous company, had seen to it that they knew themselves well beneath her.

Truth, she didn't even know what she would tell them if they asked. She didn't know what she was doing.

Finally one of them called out, "My lady . . . I think we must return."

She whirled around, green eyes flashing. The man immediately turned beet-red, and his partner looked like he wanted to drop to his knees.

The red-faced speaker licked his lips. "We were instructed to let you wander as you wished, but I fear this is too far. Forgive me, Lady Laurentii, but you seem to be running away."

Amusement and sympathy replaced her anger. "What if I am?" she asked. "What would you do?"

"Stop you," the man said, blushing again. He was nearly the color of her dress, she thought.

"There is no chance you would just let me get away?" she asked. "No hope that you might claim I just slipped away?"

"Amon would have our heads," the man replied.

"In very truth," his companion was hasty to add.

Flora was surprised to find that she felt kinship with these men. In their own way they were as much hostages as she. She decided then and there that if ever she was restored to her former fortune, she would buy them both out of Amon's service and give them a place in her own entourage.

"I suppose we must return then," she said, and duly, she headed back. The men turned to accompany her, relief visible on their faces.

"What are your names?" she asked.

"I am Beeri," the red-faced man answered. "This is Imram."

"I am indebted to you both," she said.

"Beg your pardon, lady, but what for?" Imram asked.

"You might be boors, and you are not." She paused and took a moment to look each man in the face, confirming her impression of them. "I like you both. You are frank, and honest. Gentlemen."

Beeri blushed more deeply than she had known it was possible for a man to do. "Please, ma'am. We are slaves."

"That makes no difference. A man is a man. Every man reveals himself by his conduct in the place he is in. That is a wise saying. Remember it."

"If you please," Beeri asked as they fell into a relaxed gait across the sandy plain toward the oasis, "why did you run just now?"

"I'm not sure," Flora confessed. "Except I cannot stay in that tent a moment longer. There is a face woven into it, and I cannot live under its gaze. I will tell Amon he must give me somewhere else to sleep."

The men exchanged troubled glances. She caught the look. "What is it?"

"I do not think the master will let you move," Beeri said slowly. "He told us that if you asked, we were not to escort you to any other tent."

She frowned. "Why? What does he care where I sleep? He seems happy enough to give me the run of the rest of the camp."

Imram shrugged. "*Why* he cares we do not know. Only that he does."

Flora frowned, troubled. She would rather sleep outside, under the stars and exposed to the elements, than under the gaze of Kimash for one more night. She thought now that the strange funk she had been in since arriving in Amon's camp had to do with the oppression of that gaze—though she had not been aware, it had darkened her spirit and kept her in despair.

"What is he playing at?" she asked herself.

"Ma'am?"

She looked at Beeri, puzzled, before realizing she had spoken aloud. "I'm sorry. I was talking to myself."

Beeri cleared his throat. "If the opinion of a slave is of any value to you . . ."

"Of course it is," Flora interrupted. "I have already told you I see you as a man, no more and no less. And I think you a good one. Tell me what you think."

"The master fancies himself a student of religions . . . of gods and their devotees. He worships several himself, and studies many others. You are a curiosity to him."

"Go on," Flora said. This much she already knew—but until now, she had not given much thought to her value to Amon outside of what financial gain he might get from her.

"You were born a Hill Woman," Beeri said, and paused, turning deep red again.

"That is not an insult," Flora said, slightly exasperated. "Believe me, you could say far more scandalous things about my birth. Go on."

"Born, that is, into the religion of Kimash. But you did the rare thing . . . some say the rarest thing . . ."

"Yes, I converted. In truth, I ran from the god of my ancestors to the true God, who has chosen the Holy People to himself. I know all this."

She gentled her voice, realizing she was berating the poor man when she did not mean to. "I'm sorry. Patience is not my chief virtue. Go on."

"I believe the master wants to know if Kimash still has claims on you. If, after all, he might be stronger than the Great God."

"You cast the demon out of Mashi," Imram cut in. "It troubled the master that you should have such power. He thinks the Great God weak and Kimash strong, yet you cast the devil out with the Great God's name."

The thought that she might be a pawn in a game Amon was play-

       RACHEL STARR THOMSON

ing with the gods was new to Flora, and it made her deeply uneasy. Her faith in the Great God's power remained unshaken—but she was not so sure he would come to her aid if she needed him now. Essea had been her access. Her proof of her sincerity and desire to worship him. The prayer hall at the center of the community was the closest she had ever come to the Great God's presence; the temple was forever barred to her. The Teacher's voice was the clearest she knew of the Great God's teachings.

With all that gone, she no longer knew who she was. Her birth proclaimed her spawn of Kimash.

And all of that, she realized with a suddenness that knocked the breath out of her lungs, was why Amon was so interested in her.

"My lady?" Beeri asked, reaching out to catch her as she stumbled.

"I'm all right," she said. She gripped his strong arm for a moment to study herself and then tossed her head back, striding forward again on her own power. She was all right. She had to be. "I only stumbled a moment."

She saw Beeri and Imram exchange a glance. She chose to ignore it.

Back in the camp, she paused outside of her tent and considered giving up this foolishness. It was only a woven idol, after all—a mass of thread.

But she couldn't do it. Standing outside the thick tent sides, her entire being rebelled against going back under that gaze. It was as if a veil had been lifted, and she'd seen the weaving for what it was—the truly malevolent gaze of a god who wanted her back.

Throughout the camp, Amon's slaves were at work preparing meals and caring for camels and equipment. Flora stood at loose ends for a few minutes in the street made up of rows of tents and then decided just to sit in the dirt. A flat rock close to her tent—her former tent—made a fair enough seat.

Beeri and Imram exchanged another glance and took up their stance on either side of her, arms folded.

She looked up at both of them and smiled to herself. They didn't look like jailers. They looked like bodyguards.

Yes, if she ever had the chance, she would see to it that they changed employers. She wondered about their own stories. It occurred to her that Beeri, especially, spoke like a man with some education and gentility. He was not the usual kind of slave.

She pondered whether it would insult him if she asked. The flush had only just faded from his cheeks from her other indiscretions. She'd never seen a warrior so sensitive.

The day went past. Flora remained on her flat stone. The guards remained at their post. As the sun rose overhead, she asked Imram to fetch a veil from inside and covered her head with it.

"It's, er, nice in there," he suggested when he handed her the fringed covering. "Cool. And the master had it decorated so nice."

"I won't go back in there," Flora said matter-of-factly as she tossed the veil over her head. "Thank you, Imram."

Another glance between them.

Hours passed.

Flora earned the outright stares of every slave that passed by, becoming more and more frequent the longer she sat outside. She began to suspect some of the slaves were coming by just to see her. Beeri started glaring at them, and one or two he verbally warned off. They scampered away but were soon replaced by others.

The sun began to sink. A chill settled over the desert. Flora wrapped the veil around herself, and without a word, Imram disappeared into the tent and reappeared carrying a blanket. He wrapped it around her shoulders.

She smiled at him. "Thank you."

He turned nearly as red as Beeri, muttered something like "say nothing of it," and went back to his post.

A steward walked up the row of tents and stopped to stare at Flora. She straightened her back a little.

"Yes?"

"They said you were sitting outside, but I . . ." the steward caught himself and cleared his throat. "The master requests your presence for dinner. He says you should wear the blue dress."

"It's in the tent, I suppose?"

"Yes."

"Tell him I will come, in the red dress. I will not go back into that tent."

The steward started to protest, but she withered him with a glare, and he scuttled away to report back to Amon.

"Mistress, are you sure . . ." Beeri began.

She was touched by the protectiveness in his voice, and she reached for his arm as she stood. Her legs ached from the hours seated on the ground. "Thank you for your concern for me, Beeri," she said. "But on this I will not bend. I want your master to know I'm serious."

"He can hardly miss that," Imram muttered.

<hr />

Amon's look at Flora when she entered his tent again was one of disapproval. She glanced down and slapped the worst of the sand from her dress.

"Is that how you take care of my gifts?" he said. "You are covered in dust."

"We are in the desert, Amon," Flora said. "Everything is covered in dust."

She sat. He narrowed his kohl-lined eyes, neither touching the food spread before them nor inviting her to do so. Accordingly, she reached for the biggest fig on the table and took a bite, holding his gaze.

"I told you I wanted you to maintain a distinction between yourself and the slaves. Station matters."

"I did maintain a difference. I strutted around in this dress all day."

"I am told you spent your afternoon sitting on a rock outside your tent."

"I did."

He closed his eyes for a brief moment. "I suppose you had some reason for this display?"

"The tent is not to my liking."

He smiled thinly. "You remained in it all last week, when it was nothing but an empty cell with a mat. Today I had it outfitted with every luxury for you."

"Hardly every luxury," she said with a small laugh. He did not crack a smile. She cleared her throat. "You had it outfitted beautifully. I could not ask for better, considering that we are on caravan and your resources are limited."

That seemed to placate him a little, but he frowned and said, "Then why do you say it is not to your liking?"

"The tent itself is the problem," she said. "I remained in it last week, yes, for you would not let me out. But I will not spend one moment of my own choice under the gaze of Kimash. Why did you place me there, Amon? Under the image of a creature I detest?"

At that, Amon raised a wine goblet and took a long, deliberate sip. When he set it back down, he fixed his eyes on hers and said, "That god has claims on you. You were born into his people."

"But I left them," she said. "As you well know. I was a child when I disavowed the worship of Kimash and turned to the Great God. You are an attentive man, Amon. I do not think it is an accident that you have made of my tent a shrine to the god I rejected."

He took another drink. She waited for an answer.

"To many, the gods are a convenience," he said at last. "To be worshipped or tossed aside depending on the expediency of the moment. Many, I think, do not even believe in them. Not in any way that deserves to be called belief."

"But I am not one of those," Flora said.

Amon nodded. "You intrigue me. I told you as much before. I have never seen a worshipper of the Great God so ardent as you, and yet he can have no real claims on you. Certainly not the claims of blood. Your kind are not even allowed in his temple."

Flora chose not to answer that.

Amon continued. "I wish to know what the gods will do with one such as you. I am like you, Flora, in one important way—I believe very ardently in the gods. They are real, and they direct much that happens in the world. But unlike you, I think the so-called 'Great God' least of the pantheon. Kimash, in particular, is a greater."

Flora's hands shook with anger and passion. "You speak a fool's words. The Great God has no equals."

"I know history," Amon said, "perhaps better than most of the People. Thus I know that the 'Great God' was great . . . once. But now he is old. Old and feeble, and irrelevant."

"And yet he cast a demon out of one of your slaves," Flora said.

"You did that." Amon fell silent, regarding her with a piercing eye. "I am not sure how. You are a conundrum, Flora the Unlucky: you have chosen one god, and another has chosen you. I want to see what happens now that you are here, in a place where Kimash is honored and the Great God is not."

Her face burned, but she did not answer.

"All of that," Amon concluded, "is why I will not allow you to switch tents. You are a captive, Flora. You should be grateful for any shelter at all."

"I will not go in," she said.

He raised an eyebrow. "And tonight?"

"I will sleep outside."

She could see anger in his eyes. He was not, she thought, accustomed to being thwarted.

"I should let you," he said. "If you scorn my shelter, then I should scorn you. Sleep outside the camp, then . . . without bodyguards. I should leave you to the jackals and the bandits and see what becomes of you in the morning. Oh, there are bandits . . . there are always robbers circling a camp like this, looking for stragglers they can pick off. You should know that."

"I do," Flora said, ignoring the prickles of fear at what Amon suggested. "I also know I am of too much value to you for you to follow through on that threat—you would lose far too much should a bandit 'pick me off.'"

He looked away. She saw his nostrils flare as he gained control of himself. A marvel of self-mastery, Amon was—like all the gods and great men of the Southern Plains.

Suddenly deciding to exercise her will, Flora stood. "I thank you

 RACHEL STARR THOMSON

for dinner. I have had enough and will go now."

His lip curled. "To sleep outside."

"Yes."

He cast a scathing glance at her. "You are going to ruin that dress."

She gave him a smile—one she knew would make most men weak at the knees. "I did not ask for it," she said. "Good night to you."

CHAPTER 11

The wooden posts holding up a wide platform in Avia groaned as the slaves ascended the uneven ladder to the stage. The slave market sat in the middle of a small amphitheater packed with men and a few women—soldiers, merchants, nobles and stewards, politicians and ships' captains. Overhead the sun burned in a clear blue sky.

Alack stared out at the crowd as frightened tribeswomen jostled him from one side and the other. Sweat poured down his back; the platform offered no shelter from the sun. They had passed the last several nights without sleep. The first night, wailing and crying over the dead man did not cease even as the hours dragged on. He wondered who the man had been—a warrior, a chief, his body now tossed into the sea after his death in the bottom of a slave pit.

The clamor of voices jumbled through the heated air—the slave auctioneer presiding, the crowd yelling answers. All spoke a language or languages Alack couldn't understand; in the confusion, he could pick out a word or two of pidgin but was too hot, too exhausted, too bewildered to interpret it. Not even the slaves were browbeaten enough to keep quiet. The women chattered to each other in their own tribal tongue, and Alack wished more than anything that he could sink down below the noise and find a place to sleep. He cast a longing glance at the shaded sand below the platform where he and the others stood.

His only forewarning came when Kol Abaddon drew himself taller than Alack had seen him since he last preached near the well in Bethabara.

He opened his mouth to ask what was happening, but before he could stutter out the question, Kol Abaddon seemed to grow even taller and began pushing his way through the tightly packed mass of slaves, and then he somehow strode completely past the guards with their swords and pikes and climbed the auctioneer's box.

Alack found himself gaping like a fish instead of asking anything. The slaves seemed to know he was supposed to be at his mentor's side, and they parted to make way for him as he tripped forward. The guards, as bewildered as Alack, stopped his way with the shafts of their spears. But at least he was close enough to see clearly.

Kol Abaddon stood tall on the auctioneer's box, and for some reason the auctioneer stood down. The prophet's aura had changed—like a sky full of electricity waiting to loose a storm. And everyone around him cowered in recognition of the change.

The noise died down for a moment as the crowd took in the sight of the wild-eyed, bearded man standing over them, and Kol Abaddon's booming voice filled the lull.

"Hear me!" he thundered. "Men of the Westland, I am the prophet of the Great God in the Sacred Land. I have a message for your king. Take me to your king!"

Silence lingered for one incredulous moment, and then the crowd broke into laughter, catcalls, and jeers. The guards left off blocking Alack and made to arrest the prophet before he could speak another word.

They didn't get there fast enough.

 RACHEL STARR THOMSON

"Do you mock heaven with your laughter?" Kol Abaddon called, and Alack's knees shook at the way the prophet's voice carried into the farthest reach of the amphitheater with clarity and power. "Then let the heavens return your courtesy."

And the laughter trembled into cries of fear—

For the sky was no longer blue.

Dark, thick clouds swirled overhead. Lightning flashed and flickered, and a boom of thunder so loud it shook the platform crashed. The tribeswomen covered their ears, wailing in fear, and Alack saw many of the Westlanders in the crowd doing the same.

And yet, Kol Abaddon's voice could still be heard.

"Who here can take me to the king?" he demanded.

Alack searched the crowd and saw a small contingent of soldiers gathering, wearing the royal crimson and gold. They fell into formation and marched toward the stage as another crash of thunder made the stone seats of the amphitheater tremble and crack. A bolt of lightning crackled through the air and split seven ways, forking out over the amphitheater and eliciting screams.

Alack tried to push his way forward as rain began to pelt down, but the guards had come to their senses and shoved him back with a wooden shaft to the gut.

"Kol Abaddon!" he cried out.

The prophet glanced Alack's way. "He's mine," he said sharply. "Let the boy come."

The guards glanced at one another, spears still crossed in Alack's way, and then reluctantly stepped back and cleared a path for him. He walked between them, out of the knot of tribespeople, and stood beside the box where Kol Abaddon commanded the attention of everyone in the amphitheater. More and more people were crushing their way in as the storm overhead continued to grow in intensity. Wind whipped Alack's hair into his eyes, and he struggled to stay upright.

The soldiers reached the base of the platform, and one shouted up at Kol Abaddon, "In the king's name, stop this storm!"

Alack's eyes widened as another crack of thunder shook the platform so violently that he thought it might break. The soldier took a step back, his eyes darkening with anger and fear.

"You are under arrest!" he shouted, voice hoarse with trying to be heard over the wind and rain. "Come down off that platform!"

"No," Kol Abaddon said calmly, and behind him lightning struck somewhere beyond the amphitheater. Alack heard screams and shouts from the streets of Avia. "I remain here until you agree to conduct me safely to the king. I bear a message from the Great God for him."

The soldier opened his mouth to spew an angry response, but this time lightning struck the ground in front of him, knocking him off his feet. He sprawled into his companions and got up again with new respect—and new terror—in his eyes.

"You are a god yourself!" he declared. "Come off that platform; we'll conduct you safely to the palace. If the king will see you is your own business."

"He will see me," Kol Abaddon said. He gestured to Alack. "The boy comes also. He's under my protection."

The darkness of the clouds dissipated just a little, and the wind cut back its ferocity even as the rain lightened. The crowds in the amphitheater were regaining their composure and their feet.

Men and women with pockets and purses full of money to buy away the huddling, frightened mass of humanity on the platform.

A sudden wild inspiration struck Alack, and he shouted at the soldiers, "And all these! The tribespeople are under our protection!"

     RACHEL STARR THOMSON

Kol Abaddon shot Alack a look that would have melted lead, but he did not say anything.

"All these," the soldier agreed. "We will conduct you safe to the palace. All of you."

And with those words, a ray of sun broke through the clouds.

Alack gazed at the sky with his mouth open as the guards herded the would-be slaves down the uneven ladders to the ground, and the soldiers organized them into something of a march column. But this was not like being led through the streets from the docks to the slave pit; these soldiers kept a respectful distance and suggested rather than forcing their way. Kol Abaddon called his name, and Alack forced his attention away from the sky and scrambled down the ladder to join the protected formation.

He wanted to believe he had just done something great.

The truth was he didn't feel like he had done anything at all.

——✦✦——

Leaving the villagers behind, Rechab's thoughts raged through the night shadows on her way back to the tent, until at last she burst inside and faced Aaron, his face pale and angry in the light of the oil lamps. She pulled herself up short. She had hoped for comfort from him. But his eyes were thick and wild with torment. No shred of comfort was there for her.

"They do not trust us," she said. "They did not come because they do not trust us. But how can we leave without helping them?"

"We can't," Aaron said, his voice tightly, dangerously controlled. "Of course we can't leave without helping them. What is happening here is wrong, and we can stop it. We must stop it."

"But how?" Rechab asked, her eyes pleading. "How, if they won't let us?"

A muscle in Aaron's face twitched. "They are not free to trust while Azeda is still in power."

"What then?" Rechab asked.

"We can take Azeda out of power," Aaron said.

She blanched. "How?"

"Through seeing justice done," Aaron said. "You know the law. Eye for eye. Tooth for tooth. Blood for blood."

Something in Rechab's core grew hard, and she swallowed. Her mouth went dry. "But the people won't come and accuse him."

"Not while Azeda and the elders are the judges," Aaron said. "We should have known they would not. No, we would have to bring another court to bear."

The dryness got worse, the hardening harder. It was one thing to use money to try to change things. What Aaron was talking about sounded more like using the sword.

"We cannot kill him, Aaron. Judges are supposed to come from among the people. We are outsiders."

"But nothing here is being done as it should be done!" Aaron said. His voice broke, frightening her.

What was this about, really?

What did this place mean to him?

He forced it back to a tightly controlled flat line, but he paced like a tiger, like the demon-possessed Hill Man. "The court system is supposed to work, but it is broken. Justice cannot be done within it. We can put things to rights. We *should* put things to rights."

"I don't know," she said. "What you're talking about—it's not what

 RACHEL STARR THOMSON

we came here to do."

Please, Aaron, she wanted to say. Be calm.

"We came here to help these people, as they asked us to do," Aaron said. "And we are deep in this now. Flora's money is deep in it. We can't just leave the job undone."

She put her hands to her temples. She felt like a fox that had chased something down a hole and discovered too late that the thing she had cornered was a poisonous snake.

"I don't know," she said again.

"Rechab!" He stopped, every muscle quivering. "Remember the beggars! Remember the maimed women, the children who are slaves. Remember the greed in Azeda's eyes!"

She lifted her own voice, yelled at him. "But you can't just kill him!"

Realizing that others might hear, she dropped her voice. She reached for him, put her hands on his muscled brown arms. He tore himself away, but she reached for him again. "Aaron, please! For me. Be still. Think about this."

He stared into her eyes, and as he did, the torment began to subside. His breathing, fast and labored, started to slow. So much depth in those green-brown eyes—so much passion, and so much pain. He looked suddenly like a child who has whipped himself too far into a frenzy to come back on his own, and Rechab's heart bled for him.

She touched his face. "Aaron."

He raised his hand and covered hers. She felt his jaw twitch under the rough skin of his cheek. "Rechab, I must do something," he said.

"I understand," she said, though she didn't. She understood only that all of this meant something more to Aaron than she had realized. That in these people he saw something more than a cause. But exactly what it was he saw, she did not know.

It scared her.

He scared her.

"Do you understand?" he asked plaintively. "Azeda—men like him—are evil. They are everything that is wrong with this land."

"We'll beat him," Rechab said. "Somehow."

He nodded, but the openness in his eyes had lidded shut again, covered with something she couldn't penetrate. Tears suddenly blurring her vision, she turned and ran into the night.

Moonlight cut a path before her till she stood at the head of a valley, and then she stopped, frozen in horror.

Before her, ghostly in the desert night, an army too vast to count swarmed across the desert. In the vision they were led by a man with a crooked, scarred face.

And at his side: Alack.

Leagues away, over the sea, a shepherd boy rode in an oxcart toward a palace while a king in his throne room died.

Sabrus Caelius had the king's trust. His utmost confidence. He was, after all, the brilliant general of the most powerful army in the world. He sat at the monarch's right hand and listened as politicians droned on with the reports of the day.

Outside, the sky grew black, and thunder and lightning invaded the bright day with such ferocity that a piece of the roof crumbled, and then crashed in, forcing the politician on duty to jump aside. Rain and wind pelted through the opening, the wind a howling darkness above. Chaos reigned in an instant. Shouts and screams sounded from outside

     RACHEL STARR THOMSON

the throne room, and guards ran to attend to the hysteria while the king shouted orders.

Aulus Marius, king of the Westland, turned to Sabrus with his face pale. "What is happening?" he asked.

Sabrus stabbed him in the back.

Marius gasped once and lurched forward, falling on the marble floor with as little ceremony as a mercenary dead in battle.

Only three guards remained. Their faces drained of blood, and they stared wide-eyed at Sabrus.

"Your allegiance belongs to me now," he said, wiping his knife and sheathing it. On the floor, the king labored for his few last gasps of air.

The guards did not contest the truth of his words.

If the king had ever asked them, they might have said that they knew the son of Caelius would take the throne. And if they had been very honest, they might have said it made little difference to them who sat in the highest seat of the Westland, but even they knew Sabrus would bring change, reward, riches and vision. The Westland's military, with its thousands of militia and mercenaries, made it the mightiest nation on the earth.

The king had done nothing to realize its potential, and Sabrus would.

So the king of the Westland died while his guards silently changed their allegiance, and the mightiest general in the world became the earth's most ambitious king.

Outside, the storm stilled. Clouds remained, still darkening the sky, but the rain fell only lightly, splashing off the marble in front of the dead man and mingling with his blood.

The doors of the throne room had not been closed as guards rushed out to bring order to the chaos. Now, as they returned one by one, they paled in the open doorway.

Sabrus stood with his arms folded and waited until they bent the knee, as was inevitable, as was right.

⸻ ✦ ⸻

The oxcarts bumped up the narrow, rutted streets to the palace, splashing through the rivers of rainwater that suddenly ran through the city. Dark clouds still blotted out the sunlight, and a light rain fell, plastering Alack's hair to his face and making even more of a muddy tangle of Kol Abaddon than was normal for him.

"Something has happened in the palace," Kol Abaddon said quietly. "The king is dead."

Alack started. "What? But our message—"

"A new king has taken the throne. We will deliver it to him."

Alack's head swam. "How is that possible?" he asked. "Shouldn't there be—"

"Some kind of process of succession, yes, but this time succession has been swift. Easy."

But Alack closed his eyes and saw blood.

It was all he saw. Blood, thick and dark and washing the land in death.

A hand on his shoulder. Kol Abaddon, staring at him with knowing eyes. "I did not say the consequences would be so swift or easy."

Alack stared back at his mentor, hardly noticing that the tightly packed streets had opened onto a wide street that curved in front of the palace, and that the palace itself, with a columned portico swarming

     RACHEL STARR THOMSON

with guards, lay before them—a breathtaking edifice sixty feet high, all marble and bronze and gold and stone. Oil torches had been lit to combat the day's sudden darkness.

Alack felt sick to his stomach as the oxcart lurched to a halt, and he lifted his gaze to the palace in the rain. The dark red had passed from his eyes, but he felt as though he could smell it—as though the blood had baptized him and now the stench would go with him everywhere. The stench of judgment and of death.

A hurried conference between soldiers transpired, and then the man who had ushered them here marched to the oxcart where Alack and Kol Abaddon waited and said, "You will have your audience with our king."

"Indeed, we will," said Kol Abaddon.

They stood in the throne room a mere thirty minutes later, passing through bronze doors fifteen feet high that had Alack craning his neck to take in their grandeur. The guard gave them no opportunity to clean up. Just as well. Alack felt more comfortable in his own grime and drenched in the Great God's rain than he would have felt fancied up for the occasion. Alack had left the oxcart sputtering something about the others—who sat packed in half a dozen other carts on the broad roadway behind them—but Kol Abaddon said, "Leave them," and for once, Alack listened.

The man who now prowled on the floor before the throne—rather than sitting on it—wore a scar that cut across his face and left it crooked and cocked. He seemed familiar to Alack: he felt as though they had met before, even sat and talked. Like he'd seen not only the man's scarred face and crooked expression, but something of his heart and mind—his cruelty and ambition. His eyes were bright and quick, even shrewd. His body was all brawn, his shoulders and arms massive.

"Sabrus Caelius," the soldier announced. "King of the Westland."

Alack's eyes riveted to a spot on the floor where the marble showed stains of pale pink, with dark red and black in the deeper patterns of the rock. Someone had tried to mop up the blood spilled there, but the stone remained accusing.

A look of expectation in the king's glaring eyes reminded him that protocol existed for moments like this, and he hit his knees hard on the marble floor. Only to realize that Kol Abaddon had stayed standing, and he alone was making obeisance.

Even though kneeling was the expected thing to do, he felt like a fool.

Kol Abaddon gave him a look that said "Get up," and as Alack scrambled to his feet, the king spoke.

"I am told you are prophets." He waved his hand at a hole in the ceiling through which rain was still falling, splashing off the floor where the marble was stained. "That you conjured up this storm because you have a word for me from the Great God of the Holy People."

"We do," Kol Abaddon said. Once again he looked at Alack, who fidgeted. What did Kol Abaddon want from him?

"So speak," the king said.

To Alack's shock and horror, Kol Abaddon stepped back.

Leaving Alack front and center.

"The boy carries the word," the prophet said.

The king's eyes—steely and grey in his crooked face—fixed on Alack. "Tell me, boy, what does the Great God have to say?"

Alack felt as though all the blood had drained from him and was pooling in his feet. He had no word from the Great God! What was Kol Abaddon trying to do to him? Or had he simply failed to hear something he was meant to hear? All this time, had Kol Abaddon been trusting him to understand something he had totally missed?

　　RACHEL STARR THOMSON

He opened his mouth to say something, anything, but a stammer was all that escaped.

The crooked man looked amused. "I do not have all day," he said.

Alack meant to apologize.

He meant to back away, get on his hands and knees, and beg forgiveness for wasting the king's time.

Instead he said, "I see a man."

The image materialized before his eyes seconds before he spoke the words, and he let the words form and speak themselves in accordance with the vision. His voice did not sound, in his own ears, like it belonged to him.

"I see a man with a crooked face," he said. "He is the strength of armies like fire, and he will march on the Sacred Land. His ambition is hungry and his armies like the dust of the earth for number and like jackals for their cruelty."

His face flushed as he spoke. He could see this very man standing on the brow of a hill. In a plain below him stretched out thousands upon thousands of armed men, shining below the sun. And there would be blood.

His eyes filled with tears. "He will lead his armies against the Pleasant Land and overrun it. This is the word of the Great God."

Alack closed his mouth and glanced, almost in spite of himself, at Kol Abaddon. In the prophet's eyes he saw the last thing he expected.

Sympathy.

Sabrus let out a loud, grating laugh. "Good!" he said. "Excellent!" He rubbed his hands together and slapped Alack on the back, nearly knocking him off balance. "You are the sort of prophet I like. Tell me, boy: will my conquests extend beyond the Sacred Land?"

Alack's eyes were still full of tears; he couldn't see clearly. "You will overrun the world," he whispered.

The new king of the Westland slapped the shepherd boy on the back once more, ignoring Kol Abaddon completely. "And you will come with me," he announced. "You will serve me as my personal seer, and perhaps call up a thunderstorm when I want one."

"I won't," Alack stuttered. "I couldn't."

Sabrus's eyes narrowed. "Well, then, I will blame the old king's death on you and your rabblerousing friend here, and have you executed to celebrate my coronation. After your demonstration in the market, you will make very visible scapegoats. I am told you brought others with you as well—good. The more sacrifices, the merrier the party."

Alack choked.

"My original offer stands," Sabrus said. "Your choice."

Alack looked pleadingly at Kol Abaddon, but his mentor seemed sullen and didn't make eye contact with him.

"Ha," Kol Abaddon muttered. "Some seer you will make."

Alack's cheeks flared, but there was no time to react to his mentor's dismissal. The king was waiting. "What else can I do?" Alack asked.

Sabrus turned and called for one of the guards standing in the doorway. "This boy will be staying with me. I want you to take him and clothe him and feed him something. Set the others free."

The king inclined his head to Alack in a mock bow. "There, boy. By choosing wisely, you have been their savior."

Kol Abaddon laughed at that without even trying to hide his mocking reaction.

Alack's head swam as he tried to follow everything that had just happened—and then Sabrus Caelius told him exactly what he intended

     RACHEL STARR THOMSON

to do with his new prophet:

He would send Alack as his own emissary to the Holy City to warn them of the coming attack. And demand their surrender.

A startled Kol Abaddon opened his mouth to protest, but Sabrus took him in coolly and said, "You, old man, stay in the Westland."

CHAPTER 12

S abrus had assassinated his king in an opportune moment, but it quickly became clear that he had planned the coup for months. The guards in the palace chose their allegiance at the moment the change came; those far afield—the centurions, the captains, the generals of Sabrus's legions—had already sworn their support some time ago.

And three days after the king's blood spilled over the marble floor of the palace in Avia, the legions began to arrive.

They came overland—thousands of men marching across the dusty plains to the south and through the mountain passes to the north and west. They came by ship: over the Great Sea, in battle ships, guiding merchant barges laden with cargo. As tens of thousands set up camp outside Avia, the streets packed with soldiers and the markets were flooded with goods: spices, exotic beasts, curiosities. And hundreds and hundreds of slaves.

Even as the armies descended on Avia, word went out to all the cities, towns, and hamlets of Avia that a new king—nay, an emperor— was to be proclaimed with the rising of the sun less than a fortnight after the takeover. And politicians, landowners, and free men from everywhere came to the coronation.

The might that was even now assembling at Sabrus's call left them no choice to dissent.

And the riches pouring into their country gave them little reason to.

The priests and acolytes of a hundred gods came and camped in the narrow lanes of the city, bearing the images specific to their cults and burning incense as they prayed for the emperor. They huddled at the feet of statues of the Westland gods, beautiful men and women carved in marble, each one hoping that their own deity might soon rise to prominence. Worshippers gave them offerings as they passed them in the streets. And many began to pray to a new god: Sabrus Caelius, the Sword of Heaven.

The night before Sabrus's ascension to the throne, as many people as could fit within its streets moved into the city. Sabrus would be wreathed with laurels and robed from the balcony of the palace as the sun rose in the east, shining on him in its full splendor. The throngs packed into the streets and into every doorway, rooftop, and apartment until Alack thought they would use every last breath of air and leave the city suffocating in Sabrus's glory.

Alack hated it all. And yet it fascinated him. He watched the thousands of lights and heard the noise building and building throughout the darkness of the night from a ledge around the palace roof, where he had discovered a niche among the friezes where he could perch like a bird. He felt as though he was watching a world about to be born.

At Sabrus's orders, he had washed—four times—shaved, cut his hair, and donned a toga. Alack the Shepherd Boy had disappeared, a stranger even to himself. All that was left was this foreigner, out of place and out of time. The emperor's involuntary seer.

He did not even want to think about the future. Kol Abaddon's locust-like army was real. They were here. And he himself would bear news of them to the Sacred Land.

    RACHEL STARR THOMSON

Scuttling around on the roof of the palace, narrow-eyed coolies from a mysterious land far to the east—or so Alack had been told when he asked about them—moved wheeled apparatuses into place. Long canisters with wicks like candles balanced on the axles. The coolies aimed them at the sky over the city and waited, lurking above the night. Light was beginning to bring dim life to the sky, and the city stirred with anticipation.

He would be expected on the balcony, among Sabrus's retinue. The Sword of Heaven wanted him there, and he had quickly learned that no one denied the general's wishes. He felt completely lost here without Kol Abaddon, more like a trained monkey than a prophet—and he had no doubt Sabrus saw him the same way. Sending him back to the Sacred Land as an imperial emissary was a piece of mockery, designed to show the Holy People how little they were accounted of in the eyes of the Westland. At least he could comfort himself with thoughts of the rescued tribespeople—Sabrus had made good on his word to set them free.

He gathered his legs from the cold marble and stood on the ledge, a hand on a life-size carving of a man to steady himself, looking down forty feet to the pavement in front of the palace—now one seething mass of humanity, mostly soldiers. Reluctant though he was to join the celebration, he had little choice.

The worst part was how susceptible to the celebration he felt. He knew that as he descended to the balcony and joined the small crowd of senators and soldiers gathered there, their excitement—the excitement of the city and the legions flooding it—would grasp at his own heart and beat it faster, and he would feel swept up in something great and exciting and truly marvelous. In the ascension of Sabrus Caelius to the throne of the Westland, he would rejoice in spite of himself, because the very air in this place was rejoicing.

"A trained monkey," he muttered. "I am little better than that."

As the sunlight brightened the horizon over the sea, trumpets began to blare, round after round. They made the marble underfoot tremble, and Alack's heart leaped as he stepped out onto the balcony and saw Sabrus with his hands lifted to the crowds. Their roar joined the trumpet blasts and shook the city. The soldiers at the foot of the palace began to chant, and the denizens of the city joined in.

"What are they saying?" Alack asked an ancient senator, leaning half into the old man so he could be heard.

"They are chanting 'Emperor of the world, God of armies,'" the senator answered.

Alack looked back at Sabrus—his strong arms and shoulders, his muscled back, his crooked face. Every inch a warrior, a general. And now king.

He shivered with fear and with awe.

How many years had Sabrus prepared for this day? Serving as general, amassing the loyalty of his leaders, growing the numbers of his legions. Conquering the lands to the west and north, trading, burning, subjugating all in the name of his king while he prepared to take his place as emperor when the moment was right. And now he would move east and south and extend his empire into the deserts and the great river valleys across the sea.

Alack was far from a political expert, but he realized that Aulus Marius, the king whose blood he had seen staining the throne room floor, should have seen this coming and deposed his general long ago. Much as the king in the Sacred Land ought to have listened to Kol Abaddon and acted on his warnings.

Now his worst nightmares were taking physical shape, and Beniah did not even know it.

Well, he soon would.

Alack straightened his own shoulders a little as three soldiers brought forth a purple robe. Sabrus knelt, and they laid it over his shoulders.

A senator stepped forward and intoned a short speech before laying a laurel wreath on the former general's head even as the full splendor of the sun broke over the horizon and Avia deafened the world with her cheers.

From the roof, the rockets fired. Thunderous roars punctuated the cheers, and Alack watched wide-eyed as coins—bronze and silver coins—rained down over the people of the city. They scrambled for it and screamed with delight.

Alack had heard that Sabrus had amassed great wealth in mines to the south and had shipped it here under heavy guard. He had not dreamed the general would give it out so freely. The implicit promise: *My success is your success. My riches are your riches. Give me your lives, and I will give you the world.*

The world, including the Sacred Land.

The brief ceremony ended when a trumpeter on the balcony blew one long, high call, and the legions—within and without the city, answering to a prearranged signal—snapped to attention, saluted with a slap to their chests, and gave one thunderous shout of allegiance. Tens of thousands of warriors' voices sounded in unison.

It seemed to Alack that the sound must carry across the sea; that his old father, tending his sheep on some desert hillside, must hear it; that Rechab, serving in her father's house, must wonder what had caused this distant echo.

The ceremony over, jubilation set in. Wine poured; music blared; laughter bounced off the walls of the city and over the water in the harbor, and Alack left the balcony and wandered through it all, his heart leaping with the infectious joy of the people of the Westland and sinking with fear and mourning for his own people.

Calls from the slave market drew his attention, and drawn back by morbid curiosity, he entered the amphitheater. Only to find that amid the hundreds of new captives brought by the legions and merchant ships, he recognized some of the stock for sale.

A few quick questions and he learned what had happened: the two men among the tribespeople had sold their women and children back into slavery to pay for their passage home.

With that discovery, the celebration lost its power to make his heart leap.

Alack wound his way back toward the palace until he found the right doors and the right sets of stairs, and within the hour he sat outside the dungeon door that held Kol Abaddon. Cross-legged on the floor where he could see through the bars into the narrow cell, he said, "I didn't save them. They sold each other into slavery again."

He expected a harsh response. A word of mockery. Instead, Kol Abaddon said, "I'm sorry to hear that, boy. Not surprised, but sorry. It's a good thing you tried to do."

"They are celebrating up there. Sabrus is on the throne for good."

"You thought they might depose him? He has planned this for a long time."

Alack thought of his visions of blood and shuddered. No, he did not think anyone would be able to thwart Sabrus's bid for the throne. He was the most dangerous man Alack had ever met. And his ascendancy was destiny.

"I don't want to go to the Holy City for him."

"But the Great God wills it, so you will go."

 RACHEL STARR THOMSON

"But . . . without you . . ."

Kol Abaddon laughed. "You think these walls will hold me? I will join you there when the Great God releases me. As he will. I have been in prisons before."

Alack thought of Kol Abaddon blinding the warriors from the island, and he shook his head with a half-smile.

"You can't save people just by changing their circumstances," Kol Abaddon said abruptly. "Paying their debts, buying them out of slavery—blinding them so they can't start a battle. Salvation has to come in their hearts, or it will always happen like you saw today. They will go right back into their bondage."

"Then why did you save them? On the island?" Alack asked.

Kol Abaddon was silent a moment. When he spoke again, his voice sounded rougher. "Because the power of the Great God was there, and it suited me to use it."

"But *why?*"

"I've seen more death than I care to see," Kol Abaddon said. "And more is coming. You'll have to forgive an old man's weakness."

The sounds of celebration drifted down from above, and Alack fought down a wave of despair.

The old prophet moved in his cell, drawing closer to the door. "Go home, Alack, and remember you are the *kol abaddon* now. Sound it loud and sound it clear. Tell them what you have seen here. Tell them about the Dragon in the sky."

His eyes glinted. "The Dragon is coming. Judgment will soon overrun the Sacred Land. Tell them."

CHAPTER 13

When Flora awoke in the morning, it was to the sight of Amon's sandaled feet in the dust before her eyes. Struggling to clear the fog of sleep from her mind, she pushed herself upright, ignoring the protest of her bones against the stiffness in all her joints. A heavy blanket fell away from her as she sat up—she didn't know when it had got there, but she suspected Beeri or Imram of providing it. They had changed shifts with the night watchmen, but she knew they kept an eye on her anyway. She caught both of them checking on her at different hours of the night and kept herself still enough that they wouldn't know she'd seen.

"Is it too much to hope that the misery of a night in the desert has convinced you to bend?" Amon said without preamble. "The dry cold of a desert night is a harsh taskmaster."

"It might be convincing . . ." Flora said, shaking her thick mane of hair back and combing it away from her face with her hand. Her scarlet dress was now so dusty as to be past recognizing, something she noticed in passing. ". . . for most merchantwomen. But I am an ascetic."

Amon's lip curled—an expression she was getting used to seeing from him.

She gave her head one last shake and then smiled up at him. "One night in the desert cannot hold a candle to doing weeks of penance. Good morning."

"And what sin did you spend weeks making atonement for?" Amon asked.

"Pride."

He snorted, which she found slightly gratifying. "I had thought it might be stubbornness."

"That is only a sin under certain circumstances."

"Under *this* circumstance," he said shortly, "you win. The sight of you is causing unrest in the camp. I want you to veil yourself and stay inside for the rest of this day—perhaps the next few days."

He half-turned, then said over his shoulder, "In a different tent. No images."

She nodded, swallowing an unexpected lump in her throat and blinking back tears that stung her eyes. Relief flooded her.

Moving Flora to new quarters was the work of an hour. As coolies ran back and forth with the things Amon had ordered for her, her night guards switched with Beeri and Imram again. She smiled when her friends approached. The blanket was still wrapped around her shoulders, and she removed it and held it out to them.

"I don't know to which of you this belongs," she said. "But I'm grateful."

With a smile, Beeri reached out and took the blanket. "I hope it held off the chill."

"It did," she said. "Better than I could have held it off on my own. As for what cold did get through, it is not anything my bones are not used to."

"If I may, ma'am," Beeri said, "you are a very unusual woman."

She laughed. "Thank you, my friend," she said. "I will take that as a compliment."

In the silence of her new tent half an hour later, Flora stared up at the blank ceiling in satisfaction. No more two-headed hideosity staring down at her, threatening her—claiming her.

Here she had only a blank.

A nothing.

She sat down more heavily on her bed than she meant to. Her mouth twisted in a grimace she could not prevent.

She had won a fight with her captor, impressed her guards, and made a spectacle of herself to a whole camp. She knew she had impressed them all.

But now, alone, all she had was the emptiness of a victory won through pride and the terrible insecurity of a heart that did not know where it could call itself at home.

Swallowing a lump in her throat, Flora forced herself off the bed, threw the lid of the chest open, and began to go through the clothes Amon had chosen for her—every one finely made, luxuriously appointed, ridiculous for a wanderer in the desert. She would look like a woman fit for the royal courts in any one of these.

Perhaps Amon fancied himself something of a king.

She had to laugh at that. If he did, she had proven herself a terrible royal guest.

⸺◆⸺

Nadab the Trader slowly, gingerly opened his eyes.

As it had the last three times he'd tried, light stabbed through them so sharply that he promptly shut them again. But this time he was not cowed for good . . . he squinted one eye open and then the other, letting in a shock of white and of air and sunlight.

The first time he'd wakened and peered out at a world painted white, inhabited by strangers all dressed in white, with the infernal light piercing through his eyes into his temples and all the way into the back of his skull, he had thought he was in heaven.

It had surprised him that he would end up there.

Somewhere in the hours—or days?—since then, he had realized he was still on earth. The strangers tending him spoke his own language; the smells and sounds of the place were austere, but earthy after all. The white-garbed strangers floated in and out of the room bearing tinctures and broths and frequently humming or chanting to themselves.

He didn't know exactly when he realized this was Essea—that he'd reached the place where he'd sought to find his daughter. He didn't know when he put the pieces together and realized he'd been attacked by bandits, robbed, and left for dead in the wilderness, his servant slaughtered before his eyes. He did not know how he knew that a band of young men had found him and brought him here as they made a pilgrimage across the desert.

He did know that these people had saved his life, and that he was not at all sure it was worth saving.

That Lethem was dead was the last blow. Could anyone who depended on him survive? Had association with the house of Nadab become a death sentence for all but the master himself?

With one eye shut and the other open just a slit, he carefully scanned the room where he lay. He could see his body, stretched out and dressed in white like everyone else. His hands looked thinner than

     RACHEL STARR THOMSON

he remembered them—older. His feet, sticking up at the end of the bed, struck him as absurd.

His eye fell on a man seated patiently beside him. A tall, striking man, his thin hair and beard nearly white though his face did not seem old. A wise man, Nadab thought, exuding patience and learning. And a righteous man.

He opened his mouth and croaked, "Essea?"

"Yes, that is where you are. I am glad you remember."

"Don't . . . know . . ."

"You have been told many times, but it is not surprising you do not remember everything. I fear you sustained a terrible blow to the head. When you arrived here—the young men brought you, you remember?— I was not sure you would survive."

He blinked both eyes slowly, trying to clear the grit away. The tall man leaned over to something beyond Nadab's range of sight and a moment later came back into view holding a wet cloth.

"Please, allow me," the man said. As though Nadab were a child, the man dabbed at his eyes. The cloth was soft wool; the water cool. It brought relief. When he finished, Nadab found he could keep both eyes open. His vision was a little hazy, but he saw only one of the room and the man—not three, as he vaguely recalled having seen on other attempts to get his bearings—and he felt, for the first time, as though he could see straight.

"How long?" he croaked.

The man handed him a wooden cup of water and helped him sit up straight and drink from it as he answered, "You have been here three weeks."

Nadab groaned and leaned back, letting a few drops of water spill from his lips and run down his chin. The man looked at him with concern.

"Rechab," Nadab said.

At the sound of his daughter's name, the white-haired man looked sad.

"Yes," he said, "we have spoken of her too. I am not surprised you do not remember—the blow to your head was a bad one, and we have sometimes given you herbs to help you heal that have likely clouded your mind. An unfortunate side effect, at least for one who wants to think clearly."

He leaned forward, placing himself clearly in Nadab's line of vision. He was unusually tall, Nadab thought. Tall and unusual in another way he could not quite put his finger on.

"Rechab was here," the tall man said. This was not the first time he had told the story. "She came to us for aid. I am deeply ashamed to say that when danger came on her heels, we did not provide her with the protection we should have. She escaped, but no thanks to me. I take all the blame—my community would have sheltered her had I asked them. I and I alone chose to betray her."

The white-haired man's eyes filled with tears. "In doing so I betrayed another as well. And for that crime, I feared the Great God had forever left this place. But then you came—you are his mercy to us. You are the embodiment of the Great God's grace."

Nadab shook his head, feeling an urgent need to correct the man. "I . . ." he tried to say.

"I know you do not see it. You view yourself with condemnation, as I view myself. I believe that you, like me, deserve to be condemned. And yet God has given us both a second chance, or you would not be here now."

"Here," Nadab croaked.

"In Essea, yes. I am the one they call the Teacher—my name is

 RACHEL STARR THOMSON

Jonah bar Kebna, but few care to know that. For many years this community has been a haven for all who seek the Great God in purity and in truth. I hope that it will be that again."

Jonah bar Kebna stood, extending his full six-foot-four height above Nadab. The trader trembled at the sight. There was something awe-inspiring about this man. He had something of the otherworldly air of Flora Laurentii, and something of her pride besides.

Thinking of Flora broke a dam in Nadab's mind. Suddenly memories came flooding back with full clarity—his home in Bethabara, the assassinations, the journey to find Rechab.

Because the high priest of Kimash had demanded that he find her.

Something in Nadab's face must have changed, for the Teacher looked at him sharply. "You are pale, my friend," he said. "What is it? What has just come to you?"

"There is . . . danger . . ." Nadab said. He stopped and shook his head, his hands shaking. His head was pounding as though it had been hit just yesterday. How was it possible that three weeks had gone by? Why was the priest of Kimash not already here, overrunning them all, demanding his price? Why were they not all dead?

"Tell me," the Teacher said.

Nadab shook his head, setting off waves of pain. As clearly as his fears presented themselves in his mind, he could not find the words to voice them.

Jonah bar Kebna seated himself again and leaned over Nadab with an urgent gaze. "What is it?" he asked again. "Can you tell me? Take your time . . . find the words."

Nadab licked his lips. He tried to find the vocabulary he needed to put together in order to make this man understand . . . about the danger. About Kimash and the high priest. About Rechab.

Instead he broke down and cried like a baby.

⸻ ◆ ⸻

Aurelius waited the promised two days and was surprised when a summons came from Beniah right on time. He had expected to be kept waiting longer, perhaps to find himself needing to nag. The summons was a good surprise and, he hoped, a good omen.

"I told you there was no need to fret so," Marah said as he smoothed his hair in front of a bronze mirror, readying for his audience with the king. "Beniah may be too besotted with love to remember his appointments, but his advisors are not. Someone has to keep the kingdom running."

"I only hope the same someones will influence the king in our favor," Aurelius answered, giving his wife a kiss on the cheek. "We need it. It troubles me how his face fell when I told him who our enemy was."

"I would not worry too much. I don't like the king's new allies any more than you do, but a crime this great, so close to the Holy City?—no, it will not be allowed to go overlooked."

But he caught the look in her eyes—Marah was more worried than she would admit.

"Will you take Shem with you?" she asked.

"No," he said after a moment. "I think not. One of the other servants will attend me."

"Aurelius—"

He held up a hand to silence her. "I know you are fond of the boy, but his sulking moods lately make him lax and distract me. I need all my wits about me today, and everyone else's besides."

     RACHEL STARR THOMSON

"He did not get into trouble. The other night, in the city."

"I'm glad to hear it."

And he was—Shem had long been a trusted and integral part of their household. Once they put this whole ugly business behind them, Aurelius hoped he would snap out of his strange moods. He relaxed a little—perhaps he had been too hard on the boy. After all, the murder of Nadab's household had hit close to home for them all. Shem had been away at the time, trying to track down Rechab on Aurelius's orders, and had returned to dark news and his master on the cusp of leaving for the Holy City to enjoin the king's help. And he was young. It was not surprising that he would be affected by everything that had happened.

Seated in the back of his chariot for the drive out of the northern hills and into the heart of the city, Aurelius watched the continuing celebrations in the streets. Smoke rose from small incense altars as well as cooking fires, and he detected the scents of narcotics—not a surprise, really. They were common to the worship of Kimash. The heady smell mingled with that of wine. Aurelius covered his nose and mouth with his mantle and tried not to breathe it in.

He was ushered quickly into a courtyard garden where the king waited among fountains and palm fronds. A beautiful, peaceful setting—but Aurelius's heart sank as soon as he came within view of the king, for Beniah was not alone.

Besides the usual handful of servants and six armed and watchful guards, he had company:

The high priest of Kimash stood on one side of him. Beniah's new bride stood on the other.

Aurelius cleared his throat as he bowed. "Your majesty." He bowed his head to both of the others as well—"My lady. Your . . . eminence."

Beniah, seated on his usual wicker throne, looked uncomfortable. The high priest was implacable and smug as ever, and Izevel was stunning—and so much like Flora that Aurelius had to stop himself from staring at her and shaking his head in wonder.

When Beniah did not initiate conversation, Aurelius cleared his throat again and began, "Your majesty, I hope you've had time to think over my request and look into how justice might be met."

"I am afraid that will not be possible."

The answer did not come from Beniah, but from the high priest, in his affected sing-song. Aurelius flushed with anger and opened his mouth to object, but Izevel—standing like an ivory statue beside her future husband—interrupted. Her voice was smooth and strong as silk.

"My uncle misspeaks," she says. "Justice must indeed be done. Of course. Your king would never allow lawbreakers to escape unpunished."

Aurelius felt placated in spite of himself—lured in by the coaxing seduction of the woman's voice despite her arrogance and the fact that she was speaking out of turn.

Her next words ended the spell.

"That is why," she continued, "there will be no retribution against the assassins of Kimash. Indeed, they were carrying out justice. That will be made clear to your people—we will send emissaries to see to it."

"Justice?" Aurelius sputtered. "The murder of an innocent household?"

"Innocent?" the high priest burst out. Anger flashed in the man's dark eyes, and his unnaturally pale cheeks flushed. "The house of Nadab is guilty of heinous crime."

"We had hoped to keep it private," Izevel continued, interrupting the priest—her uncle?—"but we see now that under the circumstances, that cannot be done. It would not be fair to you."

Aurelius's hands were shaking. "And what crime do you hold them so guilty of?" he asked.

The high priest smiled thinly. "Nadab betrothed his daughter to me. His household failed to deliver her."

Aurelius could only stammer in response. He looked to Beniah, desperately seeking help. He'd known this—Nadab had told him. But how these people could think that slaughtering an entire household because a girl had run away *just* was beyond him.

And now that he stood here, he regretted having sent Shem and other scouts to hunt her down. He remembered Rechab well. She had grown up in his city—a pretty girl, a little scrap of a thing, quiet, fearful. She had grown into a beauty and a credit to her father, capable of handling his business and his household together. In fact, she had served in his own house for a little while, as Flora's liaison.

Flora, he thought bitterly, had probably planned all along to spirit her away. It figured that all his present troubles could ultimately be laid at his sister's door.

And yet he could hardly stomach the thought of delivering Nadab's daughter to this man.

This abomination, he thought.

Beniah finally spoke up. "It just can't be allowed," he said, almost apologetic. "This is a most important alliance—this is my household, my wife, my new family, and an important god we are talking about. This household you speak of—"

"Nadab's," Aurelius said.

"Nadab's household makes *me* look a fool. Dishonors all of us, don't you see?"

Aurelius didn't. He was staring at the high priest. The man had a harem already, not to mention the use of the cult prostitutes. It seemed amazing that he cared so much about one girl.

But it wasn't the girl, not really. Beniah had as much as said it.

What was at stake here was pride.

Apparently the high priest of Kimash thought his pride worth killing for.

"We will send representatives with you to explain matters," Izevel said. Her tone broached no disagreement. "As well, they will continue to investigate the girl's disappearance. Until she is brought back, the matter is not closed."

Aurelius tightened his jaw. Pity Rechab, he thought.

Izevel broke into his thoughts. "You stare at me most provocatively, sir," she said. "Does something in my appearance bother you?"

He started. He hadn't realized he was staring.

"No, my lady," he said. "It's only that . . . forgive me, but you look startlingly like my sister."

A glance passed between Izevel and the high priest—Aurelius did not miss it. But she laughed, and placed a light hand on Beniah's shoulder. The king jumped as though he'd been shocked.

"I am the most beautiful woman in the Sacred Land," she said, "or so says my future husband. Are you telling me I have an equal?"

"I'm telling you you have a twin," Aurelius said frankly, with a polite bow. "But I think you needn't fear. My sister is a religious fanatic and passes her days cloistered in a desert community and dressing in homespun."

Beniah laughed. He seemed relieved at the change in topic. "Except when she plays merchant and pops up to plague you, eh, Aurelius? But you are right—Flora the Unlucky looks uncannily like my Izevel."

Izevel smiled, a delicate, frozen smile—one that struck Aurelius as serpentine. "This . . . community . . ."

"Essea," Aurelius said. "A cluster of devotees of the Great God who live behind adobe walls and consider themselves holier than the Holy People and more sacred than the Sacred Land. You will never see any of them here; they have disavowed the temple as hopelessly desecrated."

Another look between Izevel and the high priest. Aurelius wished he could read them.

"It is to this Essea that your sister . . . Flora? . . . has taken Rechab, is it not? At least, that is what reports tell us likely happened."

Aurelius's heart sank. He suddenly felt as though he had said too much—although they seemed to know everything already. He wished he had an ally to turn to in this moment, but Beniah had sunk back into uncomfortable silence, his ruddy cheeks redder than usual and his eyes cast toward the ground.

Then, to his utter shock, Izevel turned to Beniah with a sweet smile and said, "This Essea is an affront to you, my husband. It would please me if you would destroy it."

Beniah blanched. Aurelius held back a loud protest.

And the high priest spoke.

"Such communities are holes where rebellion spawns. It would be to your advantage to see it destroyed. If my bride is indeed sheltering there, you have your reason. Let the place and its people be cleansed from the land."

After a pause he said, "And let the woman—Flora?—be brought here. We would very much like to meet her."

━━◆◆━━

Aaron found Rechab seated alone in the sun early in the morning. She was trying to pray, but finding it difficult. The strong sense of the

Great God's eye upon her that she had felt in Essea had lessened even more, and she struggled to hold on to any sense of the God's awareness or favor after the debacle of the judgment.

He cleared his throat, looking down at her with his beautiful green eyes. "Rechab," he said softly.

She looked up at him with silent tears glimmering.

"I'm sorry," he said. "I'm sorry I was angry last night. I'm sorry I made you run."

She shook her head and managed a smile. "You didn't make me run. I was . . . overwhelmed. That's all."

"I know I made you afraid of me." He knelt impulsively in front of her and took her hand. "Rechab, I . . . I don't want you to be afraid. Of me. Not ever."

"I'll try," she whispered. Tears came a little faster and a knot rose in her throat. "I am often afraid, Aaron. It's not your fault."

He reached out and wiped the tears from her face. "The look on your face last night . . . I could hate myself for it. I promise I'll never give you reason to look at me that way again."

"Aaron . . ."

"It's okay," he said. He tightened his grip on her hand and smiled. "It's okay. And we have work ahead of us. There is so much to be done here."

"Done? But we failed. Azeda—"

"Azeda remains in power, and justice remains undone. You said it yourself; the people do not trust us. But we will give them *reason* to trust us. The judgment was not the only condition you made. There are the mines to reform—and prayers to lead. We are going to change this place, Rechab. The people will see how we care, and they'll learn to trust Flora's name and to worship the Great God. You'll see."

 RACHEL STARR THOMSON

Rechab stammered, "I want to believe you, but . . ."

He smiled. Her stomach fluttered as she looked up at him—at his strong shoulders and his brown hand waiting for her to take it.

She did, and he pulled her to her feet.

"There are caves further up in the hills that will make a good camp for us for as long as we stay here, so we can soon move out of the tents. The day begins soon at the mines," he said. "You must open for them in prayer. Like Flora would do. I have already chosen men from the entourage to begin inspecting conditions inside. Reform begins today. This place will never be the same."

"Aaron," Rechab said carefully, her nerves jangling at the thought of leading the villagers in prayer—the same villagers who had tossed all her efforts in her face the night before—"this matters to you."

"Of course it does." His tanned face darkened in a blush. "It matters that people be helped. That wrongs be made right."

"But it's not just that," she pushed. She knew she had not been invited onto this territory, but she had to know. "There's something else. This is personal for you, Aaron. Why?"

He was silent a moment, and she saw a battle behind his eyes. She reached out and touched his cheek gently. "Tell me?" she said.

He covered her hand with his for a moment before turning his back, but he said, "My father was crippled in a mine like this one."

He turned back, and his eyes were bright with tears. "The accident was an overseer's fault, but he had money so he bribed the elders, and my father never saw restitution. We nearly starved while my mother broke her back trying to provide for us and my father begged in the streets. Precious few would help us even then."

He managed a bitter smile. "My uncle Joachim took me into the mule trade, and then Flora hired both of us. I sent back enough money from her pay to support the family until they died. That was not long—they both had been broken by the burdens they carried."

"I'm sorry, Aaron," she whispered.

He smiled, this time a genuine smile. "You needn't be. You are doing a miracle here—it's like watching my whole childhood be changed. It is I who am sorry, for allowing my emotions to carry me away until I frightened you."

She smiled again. "We have already gone over that ground," she said. "Let's not tread it again."

He smiled and offered his arm. "They will be waiting for you."

"For us," she said.

⸻ ◆ ⸻

The Teacher of Essea left the infirmary an hour later, his brow creased with worry. An acolyte appeared almost instantly by his side.

"Is he worse?" the younger man asked.

"Nay . . . better, perhaps. He opened his eyes and tried to speak, more coherently than before. But something troubles him, and when he tried to speak of it, he was overcome. I have left him sleeping again. I gave him something to help the sleep come."

Thoughtful, the Teacher turned to his apprentice. "Micah, you spoke at length to the young men who brought him here."

"I did," the acolyte said with a nod.

"Tell me again what they said."

"That they came upon him and another man in the desert, stripped and beaten. They believed them to be dead and went about to prepare a grave, but before they could bury this one, the man groaned and

 RACHEL STARR THOMSON

moved just enough to show them that he was alive."

"And no one saw them collect him . . . no one followed them?"

"No one that they made mention of."

The Teacher thought back to their stories. Slowly he said, "The man just now had the frightened look of one pursued. He fears danger. An enemy, I think, on his footsteps. Not the bandits who met him in the wilderness, but someone else."

Slowly he began to walk toward the prayer hall, motioning for his apprentice to follow him. Micah fell in step with his long, slow stride.

"A man like Nadab might have many enemies. Yet, it has been three weeks, and all this time he has been vulnerable. We would defend him, but against any really powerful enemy our defense would be worth little. What better time to overpower him than this?"

"What is it you suspect?" Micah asked.

"That whoever pursued him saw what had befallen him in the desert and assumed what our pilgrims did—that he was dead. Believing that, they would have given up the hunt."

"Good news for him and for us," Micah said.

"Good, yes, but not lasting. Word will get out. Nadab is not a man of small repute or fortune, and eventually he must return to both."

Micah hesitated before he said, "Forgive me, Teacher, but what exactly is it that you fear?"

Jonah bar Kebna stopped on the dusty track outside the prayer hall and let himself ponder that question. His mind traveled back to the moments of his sharpest regret and a long conversation with another visitor—a seeker, but not of the Great God. The trader from the Southern Plains.

"The trader called Amon told me of a claim on Rechab's life that made me fear to keep her here. He said she had been sold into marriage to Kimash's high priest—and her father the man who had sold her."

Micah's eyes grew wide as the Teacher continued. "Kimash—or perhaps we should speak instead of his human representatives, for I hold little esteem for the 'god' himself—is not one to give up his claims lightly. The priests are bloodthirsty, greedy, and more powerful by the day in this land. If the rumors are true, the future queen will only give them even greater authority. I fear they—even the high priest of Kimash himself—is the enemy Nadab fears."

"If that is the case," Micah asked, "what do you suggest we do? I have heard tell of terrible servants in the employ of Kimash's priests . . . murderers in dark dress who move like shadows in the night and fear no retribution. You are right that our walls offer little protection against any truly determined invader."

"Would the king send us help?"

"The king will not take sides against Kimash. If I am sure of anything, I am sure of that. No, we must seek help elsewhere."

Micah squared his shoulders. A pale young scholar, he seemed to be wrestling courage up from somewhere deep inside. "We can arm ourselves . . . the men of the community. Our guards can train the rest of us."

The Teacher look fondly at his student. "My son, were you to train for a year I do not think you would stand a chance against the assassins of Kimash. They have given their whole lives to the taking of blood."

He laid a hand on the younger man's shoulder. "But I am proud to hear you speak this way. Your courage is good and right."

Micah nodded quickly, casting his eyes down.

"There is no reason to be ashamed. You are a scribe and a reader of scrolls, not a warrior."

 Rachel Starr Thomson

"But what then can we do?" Micah asked. "If they come after our guest, we cannot let them take him."

"No," the Teacher said, his eyes gleaming. "We cannot. We have made that mistake once already, and the consequences were more than we could bear."

"What then? Should we offer ourselves to martyrdom?"

Again tears came to the Teacher's eyes, and he clapped his hand on Micah's shoulder. "No, lad. We will flee before that."

Even as he said it, he knew that was the answer. They would have to flee—to leave Essea for somewhere they could be safe. But when? And where? Should they leave now—while the danger was only still a potential—or wait until word reached them that their enemies were in fact at their door?

At that point it would be too late.

The Teacher caught his breath. It was over. Essea would have to dissolve—with enemies as powerful as they had made, they had no other choice.

As quickly as that, his life's work had come to an end.

"Teacher?" Micah asked. He seemed to be waiting for an answer.

"I am sorry," Jonah said. "Did you ask something?"

"I asked where we would go. Is there anywhere in the Sacred Land safer than here?"

His mind ran through the options. They could go north to the mountains and hide in the high caves—build a new community there in the natural fortresses of the north. Shalem was no longer a haven for them—they would as soon run to the maw of the dragon. But even the mountains could only hide them for so long. Once Kamish knew where they were, the story would be over.

"We will have to go our separate ways," the Teacher said.

Micah drew back, shocked. "Teacher?"

"Essea will have to disband. Anywhere that we go all together, we will be easy to find and identify. Kimash will destroy us. No, we cannot stay together. We have no choice but to scatter our community and start anew—alone."

Micah gaped.

The Teacher managed a weak smile. "Perhaps it will not come to that. It is possible Kimash does not know where Nadab is. Or he will heal and move on before they can find out, and we will be left in peace."

He knew there was a chance Kimash would come after them anyway, to reward them for sheltering yet another of their fugitives. First the daughter, then the father.

But maybe not.

Maybe they would be allowed to go on.

"How will we know?" Micah asked.

"We will pray. And we will send ears to the towns and hope that before Kimash strikes, we will hear his rustling."

There was some hope they would not be forced to leave.

But deep in his heart, the Teacher knew it was a false one. The end had been written on the wall from the moment Flora came back with Rechab at her side.

Whatever else might play out in the coming weeks, Essea would soon be no more.

Chapter 14

Days passed. Each day, Aaron went to the mines to oversee the changes there. Every morning just after first light, Rechab went to the opening of the mines and said a ritual prayer over the day, the men, and the work.

"There should be a sacrifice," Aaron said on the third day. They were sitting together over a meal at noon, under the shade of a date palm.

"Excuse me?" Rechab said, startled.

Aaron put down the flatbread he had barely nibbled on. "A sacrifice," he repeated, "when the prayers are said. Sacrifices have always been a part of the worship of the Great God."

"In the temple, yes," Rechab said. "But not just anywhere, made by anyone."

"There was a time before the temple was built," Aaron said, setting his jaw in a stubborn way she had come to recognize. "When every man was a priest and offered his own sacrifices to God. I have heard the Teacher at Essea speak of it."

"But that was a long time ago," Rechab said. "There are laws . . ."

"Where?" Aaron asked. "They say the Great God gave us writings, but they are lost. Who knows how much of what we're told he said is wrong?"

He calmed down a little. "I'm not talking about sacrificing oxen or anything. Just a dove—Rechab. I can find you doves."

"Me?" she asked, even more startled and now beginning to feel afraid.

"You are the one they all look to for spiritual leadership," he said. "I think this is important."

"I don't understand why."

He chewed his lip for a moment and asked, "You are the one leading the prayers. How do the people seem to you?"

"Hard," she said. "Uninterested."

Trying to lead the people of Nachush in prayer was very like being in their homes, trying to convince them to trust Flora Laurentii. Even the three beggars who had originally come to her—lurking at the edge of the crowd of mine workers and curious villagers—seemed uneasy about the prayers.

"They don't take it seriously enough," Aaron said. "Do you know they have idols in their homes?"

"Yes," Rechab said quietly. "Many worship Kimash. There is a priestess of sorts in the village—a witch. She casts spells for them, accepts bribes on behalf of the god. It's ugly."

"And others worship Amon-Heth, and still others I don't know what. Azeda encourages it; I've heard him. They worship those gods, and they sacrifice to them. Mere words are not going to convince them that the Great God is worth honoring. A morning sacrifice will show them that we are serious."

Rechab considered it. She understood what he was saying—but

 RACHEL STARR THOMSON

still, the thought of slaughtering a dove every morning made her feel ill. She'd never even gotten used to beheading chickens for stew back home in Bethabara, preferring to let some of the servants do it.

Of course, worshipping the Great God was far more important than that.

She recalled the intensity of the Presence she had felt in Essea and how it had compelled her to declare herself a worshipper of the Great God and wholly under his protection and power. That presence had felt distant lately. Perhaps the problem was that she, like these people, did not take it seriously enough. Perhaps Aaron was right.

"There is no altar," she offered timidly.

"I will build one," Aaron said. His eyes smiled, and then his mouth did.

"How is the work in the mines coming?"

"Well enough," Aaron said. "Some of the workers have been diverted to repairing walls and supports, and we have insisted that injuries be seen to immediately. There are still areas we have not gone—Azeda is doing everything he can to block us through tricks and distractions."

He stared down at the meal spread out on the rock between them, but she knew he did not see it. "If only the people had come to accuse him. Without him stalling us we could do much more, and we could do it much faster. The people are still afraid of him, so they hide things from us as well—work against us when we are only trying to help them."

He sighed with frustration, and Rechab reached across the stone and laid a gentle hand on his arm. He startled a little, but she could feel the tension draining from him as they sat together, touching, one.

As he had often told her, now she spoke to him. "You are doing a good work, Aaron," she said. "The Great God will bless it. You will succeed in rescuing these people. Think of your parents and stay true."

He smiled and nodded. A light in his eyes deepened to fire and fixed on her, and she looked away, smiling, from the heat of his gaze.

True to his word, Aaron built a rough altar near the entrance to the mines later in the same day, as soon as the evening sun had gone low enough to allow for work outside. He collected the stones from the rocky slopes around the village and larger ones from the riverbed below, straining every muscle in his back, neck, and arms to lift them and carry them to the mines. He piled them upon one another in a simple but solid configuration. As he worked, his mind ranged into the past—beyond the deaths of his parents, beyond his childhood, into the far distant past of the Holy People when men built altars and worshipped the God who created all things.

Flora had never managed to convince her entourage to join her in her devotion, yet her example and the stories she sometimes told were not entirely without effect. Aaron's blood had always been stirred by the idea of a time when his fathers had purpose and identity beyond themselves, when they labored under the conviction of having been chosen by an all-powerful Deity.

He felt something of that now, here, and he hoped the Great God looked on him as he hauled stone and carefully fashioned the altar with some approval of his heart.

Of course, he hoped Rechab saw his heart too. The very thought of her lifted his spirits and made his arms stronger.

He worked on the altar until the sun had nearly disappeared. At last, wiping the sweat from his forehead and the worst of the dust from his hands, he walked with a tired body and a light heart back to the caves where he and the rest of Flora's retinue had set up camp.

 RACHEL STARR THOMSON

Just as he'd said, Amon was busy every morning. Flora did not want to know what he was doing, so she did not ask. She breakfasted alone in her tent or outside by the spring just after morning prayer. Beeri and Imram stood guard. Every morning she invited them to sit and partake with her, but every morning they refused.

It wasn't good to be seen fraternizing with a prisoner, she supposed. Even a richly dressed, well-fed, mollycoddled prisoner.

Still, there was no law that she couldn't talk to them.

Imram was as clearly a son of the Chosen Race as had ever lived. An old goat of a man, he was wiry and sharp-eyed, and he spoke with the accent of one who had grown up in the valleys of the Sacred Land. Beeri, on the other hand, intrigued Flora—his swarthy features and massive build were distinct to one of the Hill tribes, and something about his features was strangely familiar to her. Yet he spoke like one of the Holy People—and an educated, well-off member of the People at that.

"You are one of the Hill Folk, are you not, Beeri?" she asked without preamble as she sat by the spring partaking of a simple breakfast.

"By birth I am," he said. He stood with his big arms folded and a sword at his side. Had she been an outsider, she would have laughed at the sight of one woman guarded by two armed men. Overkill, she would have thought. But she wasn't an outsider, and in fact she knew herself—she had to give Amon credit for not underestimating her.

"And by nurture?"

"I was raised in a wealthy household in Shalem," he said. "My father before me was a slave, but our master took interest in us. He saw to it that we were educated and groomed for a better station in life."

Curious that you are a guard in a merchant's caravan, then, Flora thought, but she did not say it. Something in Beeri's tone was pained. She wondered what strange course had brought him to this place.

"How many of you were there?" she asked.

"Three," he answered, now sounding even more distraught. "Brothers. The second died in a plague many years ago. The master took all the better care of . . . of the youngest and I."

She looked at him sharply. What name had he been about to say? What name would she know, that he didn't want her to hear it?

She wanted to ask. She didn't. Instead she said, "You do him credit."

"Thank you for that," Beeri said. "Were my old master still alive, he would not be pleased at my choice of occupation."

Imram made a sympathetic sound, and Flora looked at him curiously. He was not offended by Beeri's denigration of his job. Instead, he looked sad.

"How long have you worked for Amon?"

"Six years now," Beeri said. He gestured toward Imram. "And he, twelve."

"He is not a bad master," Imram said. "Overall. Can't say I care for his gods, though."

"Has he always been so . . . diverse?"

"In the olden days he worshipped the Southern gods only. Took Kimash to get him really interested in the Hill deities . . ."

His voice trailed away. Beeri was giving him a look.

Flora couldn't take it anymore.

"You do not have to tell me anything," she said, "as you obviously know. But you both are hiding something from me, and I can't help wondering what on earth you could have to hide. I am just a prisoner

     Rachel Starr Thomson

here. And, I hope, your friend."

To her surprise, she saw tears in Beeri's eyes. He quickly blinked them away. "You have been a friend indeed, Lady Laurentii," he said. "A breath of fresh air in this place. I volunteered to guard you because I wanted to watch over you—there are great threats to you here, and even before you came, you gave me hope."

"I don't understand, Beeri," Flora said. Her breakfast was forgotten now; she looked into her guards' faces and quietly waited.

Beeri nodded at Imram.

The old man said, "It was his brother, Mashi, you threw the demon out of."

It was a moment before that sunk in. "Your brother! The youngest brother you spoke of?"

Beeri nodded, misery writ large across his face. "We grew older and he grew curious about the Hill Country and religion. Our master discouraged it, but he would ask questions of guests from the Hills. I knew he was starting to worship Kimash on his own—he wore a little amulet, burned incense sometimes. There was a witch in a street nearby and he would go to see her."

"Go on," Imram said quietly.

"When the master died, he set us both free. I set up a shop in the city, and Mashi went away to the Hill Country. The next I ever saw him, he was what he is now—a slave, out of his mind, controlled by some slathering, evil beast inside." He swallowed hard, and his eyes filled with unashamed tears. "Amon came through Shalem and bought him—because of the spirit, because Amon wanted to observe him, to use his gifts of . . . of divination, he calls it."

"Some gift," Imram snorted. "He predicts the future, he does, but he's wrong as much as he's right."

Beeri continued. "I wanted to help him—find some way to set him free. The best I've been able to do was get into Amon's service where I can at least protect him. When you cast the demon out, my brother came back. He was Mashi again, for the first time in years. I thought we had been given our way out. I would finish my term of service, buy my brother back—Amon didn't want him without the demon anyway—and we would go away and start life new."

He looked bleakly down at the sand. "And then Amon coaxed the demon back into him somehow. Mashi let him—he was afraid. I couldn't convince him that things would be better now."

Flora's eyes had filled with tears of her own. "I'm so sorry," she said.

"Kimash destroyed my brother's life," Beeri said. Bitterness twisted his voice. "With Amon's help. When he brought you here, I was afraid he would destroy you too. Well, he'll not do it on my watch."

"Thank you," Flora said.

She didn't know what else to say.

⸻ ◆ ⸻

In the morning, Rechab sacrificed a dove on Aaron's new altar. She shuddered deep within as she cut its throat and let the blood drain around the sides of the altar before burning the little body with incense and intoning her usual prayer.

"Let justice come upon our land and purge all our unrighteousness," the prayer ended, and the people lifted the amen with a little more feeling than usual.

It was true that the people seemed more attentive today—that the ritual drew their attention and made them more respectful of it. Blood, Rechab thought sadly, had a way of doing that.

 RACHEL STARR THOMSON

Aaron came to see her before he disappeared into the mines. "You did well," he said.

She blinked away tears from her eyes. "I hope it made a difference."

"It did. I believe it did. This altar will mark a new beginning for all these people. Perhaps they will even turn their own hearts back to the god of their fathers."

Rechab opened her mouth to reply but let the response die on her lips.

She was going to say, It will take more than this.

But what did she know about what it took to turn hearts to the Great God? All it had taken for her was fear and a one-time awareness of the . . . the realness of the god. In one moment in the Essean prayer hall, the god she'd always heard about had seemed to be there and to be as factually real as Aaron or Flora or Rechab herself. Maybe the Great God could use this altar and her prayers to make these people aware of something like that too.

So she just smiled and nodded.

———✦———

In the mines an hour later, Aaron held a torch aloft and descended down a long, narrow tunnel he had not seen before. He and a few others from among Flora's men were painstakingly inspecting every one, ensuring that the workers were not put at unnecessary risk because of conditions deep within the hills.

Conditions of the sort that had killed his father.

The darkness was oppressive. He shivered at the dankness of the air and a general sense of misery and loss that seemed to pervade this place.

Footsteps were coming up behind him, and suddenly someone slammed into his back, shoving him to the side into the rough rock wall. He dropped the torch as his arm crushed up against the rock, and he gave a yell of pain and anger. The footsteps rushed off.

When he snatched the torch up again, illuminating the tunnel, whoever had crashed into him was gone.

But Azeda stood between him and the exit, his brawny arms folded and his dark eyes regarding him intensely.

"Azeda," Aaron said. His arm was throbbing; the skin had been gashed by the rock.

"You should have your new team of physicians look at that," Azeda said, nodding toward Aaron's arm.

"Do you know who that was?"

"No."

He was lying, of course.

Aaron moved as though he would walk back the way he came, but Azeda stood his ground. This was a standoff of some kind, then.

"Is there something you want?"

"There is," Azeda said. "You make a lot of demands, boy, and a good show of religion. We've given you a lot of room to demand your way here."

"We agreed to—"

"I know what we agreed to," Azeda said, waving Aaron's protest away. "And it stands. But I'm a practical man—a man of business. As your demands are already being implemented, it strikes me that I'd like to see some payment for my acquiescence."

"You will," Aaron said, his nerves suddenly on the alert. "It takes time to transport gold from the mistress's mines . . ."

"Too much time," Azeda said. "You must have something with you. I want a down payment."

"There isn't one," Aaron said. "We are not traveling with goods."

"Then you ask an uncommon amount of faith from me. To let you come in here and make yourself master and priest, and all the time I don't see a penny until sometime in the future."

He stepped closer, until Aaron could feel his hot breath on his face. "And don't think I don't know that you want to undermine me, boy. You've been trying to get me overthrown from the moment you came here."

Aaron backed up a step and felt the rough stone against his back. "An innocent man has nothing to fear," he said.

Azeda raised an eyebrow. "Perhaps you should remember that yourself," he said. "What do the Great God's laws say about deception? About impersonation?"

He leaned even closer and jabbed Aaron in the chest. "I'll believe you are Flora Laurentii's representative when I see gold."

"What are you talking about?" Aaron asked, his head swimming. "Flora is with me—you see her every day."

"That little wench isn't Flora. Oh don't worry," Azeda said, tapping Aaron's nose, "I won't give it away. It benefits us to play this game, since I think you have some kind of riches to give me. But I want to see a down payment. Until then, you don't take a step further down this tunnel. Do you understand me?"

Aaron peeled himself off the wall as Azeda began to walk away, barely containing his anger.

But a stab of fear like ice cut through the heat of his anger when Azeda turned and said, "You had better make it soon. I would hate to think what might happen to your little actress if she were to lose you and your protection. Accidents happen here all the time, boy. Why shouldn't one happen to you?"

—◆—

On the third day of the sacrifices, Rechab poured incense over the altar and lit it on fire as she had done each of the preceding days. Its full, overpowering scent rose in curls of smoke as she covered her face and prayed, "Our Great God, we offer our worship and ask your protection. Purify us, O Lord. Amen."

The voices of the villagers, a mix of surly and curious, answered, "Amen."

Rechab lifted her hands and steadied her voice. Aaron had taught her this prayer—learned from Flora, he said.

"Let the sacred fire burn throughout the day and bring the Great God's eyes upon us always! Let the sacred fire purify our hearts!"

"Amen!"

And the final line—the one that quickened her heart in her chest as she thought of all she and Aaron had done and were trying to do, and as she thought of the old prophet Kol Abaddon and his terrible warnings: "Let justice come upon our land and purge all our unrighteousness."

"Amen."

She took the bird from a servant, held it a moment to still her own trembling, and cut its throat. She spilled the blood on the altar and set the bird to burning as the last "amen" sounded.

One more day of ritual done. She hoped it had accomplished something besides the death of a bird and the pricking of her own heart.

Aaron met her to escort her back to the caves. She smiled at him and took his arm, shaking her head when he offered a mule.

"I'd rather walk," she said. "Thank you."

He seemed troubled by something—or distracted?—so they walked in silence up the natural pathway of rock and sand toward the cave. She too was troubled, but she tried to distract herself by drinking in the beauty of their surroundings. The newly risen sun touched the landscape below with rose and gold and brought it to life.

"It's beautiful," she said in the silence. "Like all of the Sacred Land."

"Always most beautiful in new light," Aaron said.

"And in the last."

Their eyes met, and they smiled with understanding. He still seemed troubled, but she was glad to have him by her side. Her rescuer, in so many ways.

She was still thinking this over when he removed her hand from his arm, stepped into the pathway directly in front of her—making the sun shine around him like a halo—and said, "Rechab, will you marry me?"

Rechab stared hard at him. Had he really said the words she thought he'd said?

Red-faced, he scuffed his toe in the dirt—like a little boy, she thought, bashful and embarrassed and yet hopeful somehow.

"If . . . if you said yes . . . it would protect you. Make it easier for me to take care of you."

He looked up at her then, and she caught her breath at the green of his eyes. "And besides, Rechab, I care deeply for you. Very deeply. I love you."

He waited, letting those words linger in the air between them, peering hopefully at her.

She nodded and turned half away so she would not have to meet his eyes.

He loved her!

Perhaps, after all, that wasn't such a surprise . . . yet it was making the earth tilt beneath her feet all the same. And she? Did she love him?

Certainly his proximity to her made her feel all kinds of things she had never felt before—a kind of confusion and excitement and comfort all at once. It was a large part of the reason she could never tell him no. She loved the sight of him, tall and strong and breathtaking, and sometimes, like now . . .

She felt faint.

She must have looked it too, for Aaron darted to her side as though to catch her, and then his arms were halfway around her but she had not fainted after all. Instead she twisted her neck so she could look him in the face, over her shoulder.

She searched his green eyes, and he searched hers in return.

She thought he was going to kiss her, so she pushed him away.

He stood respectfully back and clasped his hands behind him, waiting.

A part of her heart cried, But Alack!

And another part said, But your father.

Alack was not here. Alack would not come here. He had left her—gone into the wilderness to apprentice the prophet, Flora said. And then she had left too, going into the wilderness on a journey of her own. Their paths had diverged and would not cross. That dream had to die.

She had always known it would someday.

As to her father, he had sold her to the shadows in Shalem. She did not owe him anything anymore. She would as soon go back to his

     RACHEL STARR THOMSON

authority, seeking his permission to marry Aaron or anyone else, as go to a pack of jackals and offer to sleep in their midst. She did not hate him—but she had removed her life from his control, and there was no going back on that now.

She remembered that Flora had once told her she had a choice. That no matter what happened to her in life, she would always have a choice of some kind to make—and it would be the choices, not the circumstances, that ultimately made her. This, she realized, was one of those moments: circumstances had brought her to a place she could never have envisioned coming, but it would be her own decision that made her now.

"Yes," she said. "Yes, Aaron, I will marry you."

He rose up on his toes, his face lighting with surprise, as though for a moment he didn't trust what he had heard. Then he laughed, unclasped his hands, and swung his arms at his sides. He laughed again, grabbed her hand, and bent low to kiss it exuberantly.

"You won't regret it!" he said. "I promise you, Rechab—you won't regret it. I will care for you gently, nobly. And together we will do great things."

He stepped closer and took both her hands, raising them to his lips. She smiled at him and wondered whether she did, indeed, love this man.

Then he kissed her, and she didn't wonder anymore.

— ✦ —

Flora didn't see the attack coming. The first she knew of it was the full weight of a man boring into her from behind, knocking the wind out of her lungs as he shoved her up against the side of a wagon, and then the fire in her shoulder and a fist in her hair, yanking her head back—

And then Beeri, seeming to come out of nowhere even though she knew he'd been with her all the time, picking his little brother up by an arm and a leg and throwing him to the ground. She turned, crumpling to her knees, fighting for breath, the blaze of pain in her shoulder driving deeper and more fiery as she moved. She saw the scene as through gauze.

Mashi's gaze fixed on her, full of hate, full of a presence that was not his own, his mouth frothing and hungry, teeth bared like an animal's. He rolled into a crouch, bloody knife in his hand, and sprang at her again.

Beeri's fist caught him full in the face, sending him sprawling backwards into the dust again.

There was murder in the smaller man's eyes.

He scrambled off the ground again and flew forward, and then Beeri slammed him back with another blow to the face, and Flora heard a sickening crunch through the pain. There was blood, and dust, and Beeri was sitting on top of his little brother and hitting him over and over again . . .

His little brother.

The one he loved.

Beeri was killing him. For her.

She lurched to her feet and threw herself on Beeri's shoulder. "Beeri! No!"

He twisted himself to throw her away, but she held on, stretched her hand over his shoulder, and commanded, "GO! In the name of the Great God, I cast thee out!"

Mashi's eyes rolled back in his head, and he convulsed. His face was a bloody pulp, every muscle and tendon standing out in relief as his body stiffened and tossed. Beeri backed away, his hands shaking, breathing hard—staring at his brother in confusion and grief and hope.

 RACHEL STARR THOMSON

Imram leapt forward and grabbed Mashi's feet to steady him. Others had already come running, and two grabbed Mashi's arms in a vain attempt to stop the violent convulsions.

Flora, swaying on her feet, pointed her shaking finger and said again, "Out with thee now, in the Great God's name, and never return! I claim this man for the Holy People in the Holy Name."

Mashi threw his head back and let out an inhuman shriek. His last convulsion was so violent it sent all four of the men holding him flying.

As they scrambled back to their feet and charged forward, Flora stared down at the man.

He had gone still.

She wavered, dizziness making her unsteady even as the pulsating pain in her shoulder weakened her.

She had done it again.

The Great God had responded to her command.

She noticed Amon watching—standing just a few feet away.

Mashi was staring at her with new, sane, human eyes. Eyes that showed fear and confusion.

Before she collapsed, he said one word.

"Izevel?"

CHAPTER 15

Flora did not know what had felled her—if it was the force of the spiritual battle with the demon or the loss of blood from the knife wound in her shoulder. Mashi had driven the blade deep—deep enough to narrowly miss her heart. A little to the left and she would not have lived through the encounter.

But when she awoke, she was a new woman.

Last time she had driven the demon out, she had been confident and secure in her status in the Great God's eyes. She was a foreigner, yes, and too proud and too rich and too stubborn, but she had given years of her life to Essea and been accepted there, and in their acceptance she had known herself to belong to the Great God. Only a day before, Kol Abaddon himself had recognized that. That time too, the encounter had sent her into a faint.

This time, though, she was outcast. This time, the Teacher of Essea had thrown her out for rebellion and opposing the will of the Great God as expressed through him.

This time, she had not *really* prayed in weeks.

This time too, the demon had been stronger—much stronger.

How she knew that she could not say, but she knew what she'd faced in Mashi's body was much worse than what had been there before.

This time, the Great God had no reason to let her speak for him.

And yet he had.

She had.

The demon was gone. It would not dare come back. And Flora the Unlucky knew that the Great God still smiled on her.

He had not thrown her out after all.

She lay on a mat in a tent, her eyes swimming with pain, and laughed.

The attendant must have taken her laughter for delirium. He jumped up from the corner of the tent—she hadn't realized he was there.

Several people were there.

"Laudanum," he said, "for . . ."

"Sit down," Amon commanded.

The master of the caravan rose, moved across the tent, looked down at Flora. She met his eyes.

He was angry.

"In the battle of the gods," Flora said faintly, "yours is not looking very ascendant."

His whole body went rigid, and for a moment she thought he was going to strike her. She closed her eyes against the pain pounding through her shoulder and whispered, "Come now . . . be a good sport."

"You are a fool," he said shortly.

"Hardly that." Her voice was faint, but a smile still lingered on her face.

     RACHEL STARR THOMSON

The Great God was with her.

She was not cast out.

She still mattered somehow.

And then she remembered something. The last word Mashi had said before she passed out. He'd been staring at her with fear and confusion and, she thought, recognition. And he'd said *"Izevel."*

"What did he . . . say?"

Amon glared at her a moment longer and then turned his back to her and said, "Do you know who your mother was, Flora?"

The question was so unexpected that she found herself gaping at it. She tilted her head. "My mother was a prostitute."

"And?"

"And a Hill Woman. A worshipper of Kimash."

Amon looked amused in his anger, but for the life of her she didn't understand why.

"Is that really all you know?" he asked. "Are you so ignorant?"

Her mouth and tongue were dry—she desperately needed a drink. She managed to clear her throat. "Apparently I am."

His eyes darkened—almost black. He crouched beside her and looked her straight in the eyes, and for the first time in his presence, she felt real fear.

"Your mockery has tried my patience long enough," he said. "You have cost me thousands—thousands—by destroying that slave."

"The Great God set him free," she croaked.

"Did he? Then why is he in chains now, as we speak? I had a buyer for him—a man of influence, great influence, with the new queen. You have cost me more than just money."

"I saved a man's life," she said.

His hand shot to her throat. She stiffened, but he stopped mere inches from touching her and slowly retracted his hand. She wondered what it really was that made him so angry.

And then she knew.

"You could be free too," she rasped. "You do not have to live in so much fear. This is . . . a wise saying, Amon. Freedom and slavery are all about who you worship."

The words had barely escaped her lips when the pain from her shoulder seared through her again, and she heard herself cry out in pain as everything went dark.

———•◆•———

Flora awoke in the night. She thought the wound had been cleansed and bandaged again, and she might have been given something for the pain—whatever the reason, it throbbed but no longer cut her with fire, at least for the moment.

She had been moved. She recognized the oily, skin-crawling atmosphere of the tent almost before she saw the image woven into its wall and closed her eyes against a wave of fear. Amon's interest in her had changed. She was no longer a guest—no longer a curiosity. She was an enemy, and he meant her to know it.

All through that night, she did not cease her prayers to the Great God, though it was the grotesque face of Kimash that glared down at her.

She was still at prayer when the summons came. Two of Amon's servants, broad-shouldered Southern men, parted the curtains and motioned for her to follow them.

 Rachel Starr Thomson

She rose. Relief washed over her as she stepped out from beneath the emblem of Kimash into the light of the morning sun. She had not slept since awakening to recognize it in the dim light of an oil lamp.

Her wound pained her as she walked, and she held her shoulder with her good hand to keep it from jarring too badly. More Southern guards fell in behind her. She wondered where Beeri and Imram were and if she would be allowed to see them again.

Amon stood in a clearing between the tents, ringed by camels bedecked with veiled litters and surrounded by armed men. He wore red robes, and he had painted his eyes in dark, slanted Southern fashion. He held a bronze axe with an ornately carved blade and obsidian handle.

At his feet, Joachim knelt with his arms bound behind him. He looked up at Flora, grey eyes in a grizzled face that she had known and loved for many years—her servant, and friend, and in some respects even a father.

She swallowed hard but said nothing. She would not show Amon that she was afraid.

"Welcome to a new day, Most Favoured of Women," he said.

He mocked her. Her name, Infortune, Unluck—that was the truth. Her wealth and power had come to her through curses and death, and curses and death had not released their hold on her. The sight of Joachim in danger quickened her blood and sent it pounding through her temples.

"I think you must have the wrong woman," Flora answered, "for you call me by the wrong name."

Amon's eyes narrowed slightly. He did indeed have the wrong woman—he had pursued Rechab the daughter of Nadab the Trader and caught Flora by accident. But it seemed he did not appreciate being reminded of that now, now that he had come to rue her presence so completely.

Amon broadened his stance over Joachim, hefting the axe in his hand, and announced, "I am going to kill this man."

Her heart pounded harder, the rush of blood threatening to knock her off balance. "What do you want from me?" she asked.

"What do you think I want? You are the wealthiest woman in the Sacred Land, Flora Laurentii. I want many things from you, but for a start, I want your money."

"You can't have it." She felt like a traitor saying the words, as though she had picked up the axe herself and beheaded one of her oldest friends. She wanted to look Amon in the eyes, but she couldn't tear her gaze away from Joachim—begging him to understand that she did not have the choices Amon thought she had.

He rolled his eyes. "I am tired of your games. You will do whatever it takes to transfer ownership of your property to me, and that is the end of it."

"I can't," she said, shaking her head and blinking away frantic tears. "My wealth is not mine to give."

"Then whose is it?" Amon asked, his voice dripping with sarcasm.

"Another's," Flora said. "I have given it to another."

"You expect me to believe such a blatant lie?"

This time she managed to meet his eyes. She broadened her own feet, taking her own fighting stance, though he was armed and surrounded by slaves, and she had nothing but her wits and her tongue—and those slowed by pain and whatever drugs had been given her to fight it.

"You know me well enough, Amon, to know that I am not beyond giving everything I have if the Great God asks for it. He asked for it, and I gave it. An act of worship. I have no more money than the man you hold hostage at your feet. If I had, do you think you would have found me wandering like a pauper in the desert?"

 RACHEL STARR THOMSON

He narrowed his eyes once more, considering her words. She wanted to hold her breath but refused to look that nervous. Her words were true—in a way.

True, at least, that she did not have the freedom to turn her wealth over to Amon. If she did so, she would betray Rechab and all of the retinue with her. Amon had hunted Rechab long before he ever wanted Flora; he would be no less a danger to her now, and if Flora stripped away the protection of her money, her name, and her servants, the girl would be without a shred of protection. She would place them all in mortal danger. They trusted her, and she would not break their trust.

She only hoped that Joachim would not die for her lack of choice in the matter.

"You are bluffing," Amon said. The dark lines of kohl around his eyes made his expression difficult to read. "This man will pay for your lies. And then *you* will pay—every penny I know you still have."

He raised the axe once more. Flora cried, "Wait!" Yet the axe would have fallen—should have fallen—but that a servant interrupted.

"My lord."

Amon turned abruptly to face the newcomer, a messenger who groveled in the dirt. "What do you mean by interrupting me?" he demanded.

"Please, my lord," the servant said, his face to the sand. The shadow of the axe fell on him now, and he squirmed as if he could feel it. The camels looked disdainfully on him. "I thought you would want to know the word I bring before . . . before anything further is done."

Amon's eyes narrowed once again, and he lowered the axe. "Speak."

"Word has come that Flora Laurentii is in the north. They say she has seized control of two mines in a valley some miles from here, and that she tries to bring the Great God's laws to bear."

Now the Southern trader's eyes widened in surprise, made all the more dramatic by his makeup. "When is all this supposed to have happened?"

"In the last several weeks," the servant said. "I spoke to the villagers. They swear they saw Flora Infortunatia with their own eyes only yesterday."

Amon threw back his bald head and laughed.

He turned back to Flora. "So you *have* given your wealth away!" he declared. "Your wealth, and your name! 'Infortunatia'—a worthy gift for some fool."

Fear for Rechab sliced through her, crowding out even the threat to herself, but before she could begin to find a way to cover for the girl, Amon had figured it out.

"Flora in the north . . . the trader's daughter. That is your act of worship. To pass your misfortune on to the child and try to run and leave it behind. That is unworthy of you."

"Please," she said. "The girl has nothing to do with you. Leave her be."

"Then what will I have to give the powers in the Holy City?" he said. "You have already destroyed the slave I planned to sell them. Now you would deny me the gift I want to bring. Great powers are in the ascendant, and I would be at their side. It will not be if I cannot offer a gift."

He stepped closer to her, leaving Joachim heavily guarded. "I have lost Flora Laurentii's fortune. You wish me to abandon my hunt for the runaway. You expect me to go to Shalem empty-handed?"

"Give them me," Flora said. "Keep Rechab's secret, and I will go with you willingly."

Interest, intrigue, passed across his face. "You think they want you?" he asked.

 RACHEL STARR THOMSON

Her stomach sank, and her heart lower—a rock to the pit of her soul. "They have always wanted me," she told him. "Since I was a child in my mother's house."

"And what is to prevent me simply from taking you?"

Her eyes flashed. "I would find a way to prevent you."

A smile quirked in the corner of his lips. "No doubt you would. And I should trust you to cooperate with me?"

"My word is worth more than you know," she said. "Only let my servant go."

Joachim hollered something in protest, and one of the guards kicked him silent.

"That was not part of the deal. You said only to keep the runaway girl's identity secret."

"It is part of the deal now."

He walked slowly, circling her, a jackal with its wounded prey— wounded but still dangerous.

"Do you know how I found you?" he asked. "You were seen and mistaken for the runaway Rechab by a messenger of your brother's. He was going back to Bethabara to report when an apparition of the god Amon-Heth led him straight to me."

Flora stared, trying to process Amon's words and keep a steady expression at the same time. She didn't understand.

"Do you know the story of the Adversary, Flora Laurentii?" Amon asked.

She shook her head. She did not.

"Small minds believe there are many gods," Amon said. "Even I speak of the gods as plural. But great minds know a deeper truth—that at any time, in reality, there are only two."

"One," Flora said. "The Great God is One, and only One is God."

"You parrot the Teacher of Essea with such conviction," Amon said. "But what makes a god, after all? Does not power make a god? And even you must admit the Great God is not the only power in the universe. If he were, who delivered you to me? Who nearly killed you in your hut in Essea? Whose temples and shrines dispense favors and graces and small powers? Whose spirits inhabit my slaves and drive them wild? Can you answer that?"

"The pagan gods are evil spirits," Flora countered, "small-minded creatures with no passion but to destroy."

"Small-minded creatures cannot create and sustain entire religions," Amon said, "nor can they dispense power as they will. The greatest of the 'evil spirits,' as you call them, can. And when any spirit is powerful enough, what is to stop him from declaring himself a god? Why should he not? Why should he not declare himself equal even with the Creator?"

The blasphemy shook Flora even as it angered her. Few in the world would dare to speak in this way, openly.

"You said there were two gods," she said.

"Yes. The Great God, so-called, and the Adversary." Amon walked slowly as he talked, circling her. "The Adversary—the Dragon. A great mystery lurking behind every religion, every shrine, every idol. I have traveled far, Flora Laurentii, and everywhere I have gone I have learned. I have gone deep into the mysteries of the nations and their priesthoods. So it is that I declare to you that there are not many gods among the pagans, but only one, expressed in many ways and by many names. The Adversary alone rules the kingdoms of this world."

"Why do you call him the Dragon?"

"Because he has been called so from the beginning, since before our world came up from the waters. Leviathan, the Great Serpent. He

 RACHEL STARR THOMSON

is seen in the stars, and it is his image that lurks in the darkest places of every religion and cult on earth."

"Except ours," Flora said. "Except the religion of the Great God."

"So you think," Amon said. "But I tell you, were you to enter into the most sacred part of the temple in Shalem today, it would be the Adversary you would find there."

The idea shook and disgusted her. "The People are not that far gone."

"Believe that if you wish."

"What are you trying to tell me?"

"That the balance of power is about to shift. The Adversary has bided his time over centuries, slowly gathering worshippers, slowly increasing his strength. Keeping his enemies distracted by presenting not one face, but many. But the time has come that he will show one face, and he will tear down the Great God's sanctuary and sit enthroned upon the Holy Mountain."

"The Great God is the creator," Flora said, holding her voice as steady as she could. "No upstart, no matter how powerful, can rival him."

"Have you ever observed a father and son?" Amon said. "The father sires the son and is as far above him in power as a man is above a worm. But the child grows and prospers and becomes a man, and the father withers and bends like a dry tree. And in the end, if the son would snap his father's neck, the father could do nothing against his strength. Such is the Adversary to the Great God. The Creator is old and his power is waning. Even his beloved, the Holy People, have turned their backs on him for his weakness and absence. The Adversary is a strong son and he will overpower him."

"Never," Flora said. "It shall not be."

"It shall. It cannot be stopped. The stars show the signs of it. The whole world shows signs of it. The strength of the nations grows. Shalem is full of idols and priests of other deities. Kimash prepares to take the throne. Amon-Heth brings you to me as a gift, Essea throws out refugees and defiles their own purity, and the only voice the Great God has is one tormented, mad prophet. A prophet who is more than likely dead."

"Kol Abaddon is not dead."

She didn't know why she spoke with such passion.

He lifted a finely crafted eyebrow. "You say that as though you know. Do you know something of the prophet's whereabouts?"

"I do not," she said. "But I would know if he were dead."

Amon's eyes narrowed. "Does the prophet mean something to you?"

She flushed. "He is a servant of the Great God. Perhaps the greatest such servant now living. I would give my life for him."

Amon shook his head slowly, but he did not voice his thoughts. Finally he said, "And so you ask why Amon-Heth would lead me to you. But you yourself said that the gods have always wanted you. You are marked, Flora Laurentii. You have always been marked. You—the few people like you—are at the center of the Adversary's will."

"I don't understand."

And yet she did. She knew that what he said was true. A sick feeling was growing in the pit of Flora's stomach, but she stayed in control of herself. Amon stopped his pacing and looked her directly in the eyes.

"The Adversary—he has many names. But as the Great God has sometimes called himself Love, the Adversary has named himself Hatred. And it is *you*, Flora Laurentii, you and your community of

     RACHEL STARR THOMSON

disciples and your mad prophet and your runaway little girl, that the Adversary hates. It is not good in this world to have enemies. You have the worst enemy there is."

His words chilled her. And drew up a memory.

In the darkness of the shrine. Where the air was always strangely cold, no matter how the summer hills blazed. Where the old blood of sacrifices stank. Flora, a child, hidden among the curtains, staring with wide, terrified eyes at the horrible creature barely lit by oil lamps—Kimash, the abomination of the Hill People.

She had been sure the idol wanted her and that it would eat her alive with its horrible dragon teeth.

Enmity.

Hatred.

Yes, that was what she had felt.

And the same enmity was looking coldly at her through Amon's eyes.

Through the smile that was slowly stretching across his face—a smile so inhuman that it struck chills through her, and it was all she could do to stay on her feet and not become a child before it, as terrified as she had been in the presence of her mother's god.

But as frightened as she was for herself, it was nothing to the fear she felt when she contemplated Amon's words about the Dragon.

Could it be—was it possible—that Amon was right?

That the creation would surpass the Creator, the child the father?

That the serpent from the darkness, Leviathan of old, could rise up and come into power at last?

Tears pricked at her eyes, and she turned so that Amon could not see her face. She felt his satisfaction nonetheless.

"You see," he said. "Even you cannot deny the truth of my words. So yes, Desired of the Gods. I will accept your offer. I will take you to Shalem."

"Let my servant go."

And then he smiled, and it was the cruelest smile Flora had ever seen from him. "No," he said, "I don't think I will."

He raised a hand in commandment, and as Flora watched, six of his guards dragged out two more men in chains—both of them beaten and bloody.

Beeri and Imram.

The world spun around her.

"No," she whispered.

"I asked you if you knew who your mother was," Amon said. "You, it seems, do not. But I do. She was no common whore, Flora Infortunatia. She was sister to the high priest of Kimash. Did you have sisters, brothers? Anyone older than yourself?"

"No," she said, sick to her stomach. If it was the dizziness or Amon's words or the sight of Beeri, Imram, and Joachim all helpless on their knees, she did not know.

"Then I am a very fortunate man after all," he whispered, stepping close to her, moving her hair off her neck. "And you are very, very unlucky. A priestess's oldest child is always consecrated to the god, Flora."

She knew before he said it.

Before he said, "That's you."

She knew he was right.

"Yes, you will go to Kimash. You will be worth more than my slave, more than Rechab could have been, more than your mines—though

 RACHEL STARR THOMSON

be assured that I will find Rechab, I will take her, and I will have what is yours somehow."

She closed her eyes to shut out his face. She could feel him moving away from her, turning his gaze away.

He lifted his voice. "Let it be known that anyone who befriends this woman from this time forward will be considered a traitor to me."

He whirled around and met Flora's gaze, then lifted his axe and nodded to his guards.

"Kill them."

Two guards grabbed Flora's arms, preventing her from throwing herself over the victims. She heard her own voice, hoarse as she struggled against them. "No! Amon! No!"

But there was nothing she could do.

Before her eyes, Amon's guards slaughtered all three men. They left Flora crumpled on her knees in the bloody dust, sobbing.

Not long after, guards snatched her up from the dirt, and directed by Amon, they tied a blindfold around her eyes and left her bound to a post in the tent of Kimash.

<hr>

Flora ached in the tent where she waited, bound, a prisoner. She could see, just barely, around the edges of the blindfold. Shadows and footsteps outside told her she was heavily guarded. Though she tried to sleep, sleep refused to come.

The shadows of Shalem loomed over her heart and mind. The oasis air that drifted through the tent was cool and tinged with hints of water from the nearby spring and the pool it fed. Amon's camels vocalized their satisfaction as they drank their fill in the darkness.

She blinked away tears. They trickled down her face in worn, sore tracks.

In Essea, as penance for walking too closely with the world, she had sometimes prayed with weights tied to her wrists. But even then, the call of the Great God that pulled her upward had been stronger than the downward weight. Now she felt as though a weight was pulling her soul straight down, through the ground to the world of shadows below.

She had made her soul an offering for the life of Joachim and the others, but it had not been enough for Amon. She could only pray it would be enough for Kimash.

The prospect of being returned to the monster from whom she had fled so long ago made these moments, alone, frightening and yet precious. Whatever Kimash required of her, she believed it would end in death—and so these were her last hours, her last time to live.

She breathed the cool air, smelling water and the sweetness of orange trees that grew by the pool.

The Hill People looked at the sky and saw gods. They looked to the earth and saw demons. They made for themselves idols, and they fell down and worshipped the images of all that they feared. But the Holy People taught, as their fathers had taught them from time immemorial, that the Great God made the heavens and the earth. That he named every star and turned every season in its time. The Sacred Land was his garden, his sanctuary. The sky arching overhead, full of lights, was the roof of his temple.

And in *this* temple, even if Flora was blinded against it, she could worship freely, worship the God she loved—the one she knew still heard her, still saw her, and still allowed her to call him her own.

 RACHEL STARR THOMSON

———◆———

Flora could not see that Amon sat in the shadowed corner of the tent, watching her.

What was it about this woman?

He had known Flora Laurentii for years. Hers were some of the richest mines in the Sacred Land. Imperious and terrifyingly beautiful, she dealt with merchants as one of their own—with shrewdness, wit, and a sharp eye for profit. Her fanaticism sometimes meant waiting on her while she prayed or carried out other rituals, but that only added to the power she wielded over those who came to court her favor and buy her wares. He had often suspected her of wielding her religion for that reason alone: because the reputation it gave her made her strange, unpredictable, and aloof, and so set her apart from the merchants' guild in ways that were to her advantage.

But the woman who had resided in his caravan for weeks now, faithfully praying and refusing to sleep under the eye of Kimash, wielding her wit against her host as though it were a sword—this woman who had given her riches to another and now sacrificed her life in a vain attempt to save others was no hypocrite. No canny profiteer. Her sacrifice was real. She was real.

He watched her as she stood bound to the pole, her face drawn and pale with pain and with grief. Her lips moved, and he knew she was praying. The guards lingered by the doors but would not look at her.

Amon wanted to tell himself it was because of his warning. Because they had learned from the fates of Beeri and Imram. But he knew the truth was something else.

They were afraid of her.

Worse, so was he.

Bile rose in his throat. He did not understand what he was looking at in this woman. He did not understand what he felt.

For one wild moment he considered abandoning his plan. He would not give her to Kimash—he would keep her for himself. Discover all of her secrets, and in humiliating her overcome his own fear.

But he couldn't.

He choked on his own terror.

His hand gripped the dagger at his waist. He strode across the tent, watching her stiffen as she realized someone was there, and snatched the blindfold from her eyes.

They flashed at the sight of him. For a moment they stood, face-to-face, enemy to enemy.

"Why are you doing this?" she asked. "Why bind me? I am no threat to you."

"Because your freedom offends me," he spat.

She was silent a moment, green eyes boring into his soul. "You are afraid," she said.

"Be silent, woman."

But she did not obey.

"My freedom is nothing to you. It offends only Kimash, and you are so under his control you do not understand yourself."

He raised his hand to strike her with all the pent-up turmoil he had brought with him into the tent, but he could not bring himself to deal the blow.

Instead he looked up at a guard who had entered the tent when he stood and snapped, "Blindfold her again."

     RACHEL STARR THOMSON

The servant hesitated.

"Do it!" he shrieked.

The guard nodded curtly and pulled the sash back around Flora's eyes, tying it tightly back.

With her gaze cut off, Amon relaxed slightly. Bound and blindfolded, her power was dimmed.

But he wondered if this was not a woman he held in his power. If she was something more—some kind of goddess, some child of a god and an earthly woman such as he had heard stories about.

He shook his head, feeling his anxiety and anger begin to release. Whatever she was, he would not chance dealing with her himself.

Kimash wanted her, and to Kimash she would go.

CHAPTER 16

Although he did not say a word to her about it, Rechab knew that Aaron had doubled the guard watching her throughout the day. She noticed the men lurking, pretending they weren't watching her like a hawk. Always armed and ready for a fight.

She was grateful for his care, and yet something about the increased bodyguard troubled her. As though, now that she had agreed to become Aaron's wife, she had lost all the freedom she'd known as Flora Laurentii's representative.

As Flora Laurentii herself, her conscience told her. You have had all this because of a lie.

But it was not a lie that would last forever. Eventually Flora would come back, and Aaron and Rechab would be married, and they would finish their work here and leave to establish the humble little merchant business in the south that she'd dreamed of when she set out on this mad journey.

Sitting in the shadows of her little cave, she found that she could hardly wait for that day to come. Being Flora was a demanding job, and she had decided that she was not up to it after all.

The guards were nearby, walking the edge of the limestone ledge outside the cave and looking down on the town. Only two of them—the other two were gone for a moment.

With a quickening pulse, Rechab realized she could slip away for a moment if she wanted to. These two seemed distracted by something, and she could move quietly enough to get by without them noticing her absence for a few minutes at least.

She did want to, she decided. She wanted to breathe free air without knowing that someone was counting the breaths that she took.

Smiling to herself, she gathered her feet under her, waited for the right moment, and then slipped away from the cave as quietly as the mousy girl she had once been would slip away to meet with Alack.

The evening air was cool, the setting sun lighting up the sands and the white stones on the hill slopes. She breathed deep, glad for the freedom, glad for the coolness. The guards would notice in a minute or two and come after her, but for this one moment, she had slipped the bands of Flora Laurentii and become Rechab again.

Her feet carried her along the path, downhill toward the village and the river. She meandered west, toward the water and the wilderness, so she would not actually enter the town if the guards took that long to catch up to her. She didn't want to see any of the people whose sour faces she knew so well from morning prayers.

She reached a shallow stream that flowed into the river and sat on a flat rock beside it, taking off her sandals and lowering her bare feet into the cool flow. Smiling to herself, she thought of the Great God and imagined his eye upon her—it was rare that she felt alone enough to train her thoughts on him. She had not lost her zeal to learn to worship him properly, when the time came—to seek out someone who knew more about how to honor the Great God according to his own laws and ways so that she would not always feel like a pretender.

 Rachel Starr Thomson

When she heard the crunch of footsteps behind her, she assumed it was the guards.

She had almost turned to greet them when she felt something sharp against her ribs and a low voice that she knew too well said, "Fancy meeting you alone."

"Azeda," she said, stiff, hardly daring to breathe lest he push the knife any deeper.

"Unveiled too," he said. He moved slowly, coming into her field of vision as he crouched down beside her. For such a big man, he moved gracefully—like a lion, she thought.

"It's funny," he said, keeping his voice low and congenial, "I always thought Flora Laurentii was older. You can't be much more than eighteen."

She kept her breathing steadily controlled, taking in air through her nose, not saying a word. The knife point had not moved.

"I am surprised that strutting cock you keep as a companion would let you out alone. Tell me, does he really have access to Flora's mines?"

She didn't answer. The knife pushed just a little deeper, and she gasped.

"All I want is an answer," Azeda said.

She nodded, a quick, short nod. She didn't trust her voice.

The knife pulled back slightly. "I don't understand what you're up to," Azeda said, "but here's my advice: just keeping playing your little game. You might tell the boy to make sure he does what I've asked him to do. Here . . . I'll send a token back with you, from me."

He pulled the knife away quite suddenly, took her hand, and slashed her palm.

She pulled her hand back with a gasp of pain and shock as a line of blood sprang up.

Azeda tucked his knife away, smiling.

"Make sure he sees that," he said. "I want gold, girl. I will have it, or you will pay in blood. Do we understand one another?"

Rechab hadn't said one word since he sat down—she was frozen in fear, and now fear danced through her veins as her hand grew hot.

Azeda stood. He took one last, long, uncomfortable look at her, and then turned around and strolled away toward the village. She watched him go. Three more men joined him, seemingly out of nowhere—they'd been there, among the rocks, waiting for him.

She began to shake.

How many others knew their secret?

And what was Azeda talking about—what had Aaron been asked to do? Kicking herself for her foolishness, she realized too late why Aaron had doubled her guard. It was not overprotectiveness on his part: the threat had been real.

But *of course* it was real. She berated herself as she returned up the hill, breaking into a half-run as the caves came back into view. Her bodyguard, up the hill, caught sight of her, yelled, and began to run toward her. Not one moment of this whole adventure had been safe. Danger had dogged her steps from the moment she left Bethabara with Flora, and even before. What had she been thinking to wander off on her own?

Her hand stung. She had balled it into a fist, and she kept it that way even when the guards joined her. By that time she was crying.

"Are you all right, my lady?" one of them asked. *My lady*. She wanted to laugh. That was Flora's title; these were Flora's men. She was nothing but a joke and a risk.

She wanted Aaron. She managed to say that. "I'm fine. Aaron . . . please get Aaron."

One of the guards jogged off to do her bidding while the other three, surrounding her, escorted her back to the cave. They exchanged worried looks, but none of them pushed her on what had happened.

They took her to the door of her cave and then stepped back. One of them looked at her with mild reproof and said, "You should let us know, my lady, if you want to go for a walk."

She nodded.

Aaron arrived minutes later, flushed and out of breath. He took one look at her tear-stained, pale face and burst out, "What happened?"

He was with her in a moment, gathering her in his arms and holding her against his strong chest. She relaxed against his heartbeat, not wanting to talk. She just wanted to stay here, safe, herself without having to explain anything.

But of course she couldn't. She had to tell him what had happened.

He held her for a long time and then gently pushed her away. His eye caught sight of her tight fist . . . and the blood that had seeped through her fingers and dried.

"What happened?" he asked, his tone completely changed. This was not the gentle, patient Aaron she needed, but a dead-serious young warrior who needed answers.

"Azeda," she said. She couldn't get any more out.

He took her hand and pried her fingers open—gently, but not asking. She watched the color drain from his face and his jaw go taut at the sight of the slash. It was not deep, but its edges stood up and it had bled into all the lines of her palm.

"He said . . . he said to tell you to do what he asked. Aaron, he knows I'm not Flora."

"Where were your guards?" he asked. He stepped back, leaving her alone. "Why weren't they watching you?"

"I slipped away," she said, fresh tears coming to her eyes. "I just wanted to be alone for a few—"

"It's not safe!" he shouted.

She felt as though she'd been slapped. She must have cringed, for Aaron softened for a moment—but then lost himself in his anger again.

"What were you thinking?" he said. "He could have done anything to you!"

"I know," she whispered. "I know, Aaron. I'm sorry."

He was pacing, prowling. "I'll make him pay. I'll make him—"

"Aaron," she said, finding a little courage, "don't do anything rash. Please. Right now he knows too much. He could hurt us both."

Aaron stopped and looked at her coldly. "He already has. He could not hurt me worse than by attacking you. He knows that." He looked down for a moment, and then back up at her. "He didn't do anything else?"

She shook her head. "Only threatened. Me *and* you. Aaron, for my sake, don't do anything rash."

"What do you want me to do?" he shouted again. "You put me in this position—you tell me how to handle it!"

Regret flooded his face immediately, but he was still too angry, too scared to calm down. She saw all the emotions battling in him and wanted to soothe them, but she was still too afraid herself—the encounter was still too fresh.

"Maybe, Aaron . . ."

"Maybe what?"

     RACHEL STARR THOMSON

"Maybe we should leave here," she said quietly. "Maybe we should give this up."

"We can't do that," he said, every word staccato. "We're not done here."

"But Azeda—"

"Azeda would threaten us even if we left. He has to be dealt with. I'll deal with him."

"Aaron." She looked at him sharply. "Promise me you won't kill him."

He stared incredulously at her. She dared to step closer and touch his arm. "Not . . . not like a thief, not like a murderer. I don't know what you're planning to do, but don't . . . don't do anything *wrong*."

The sky outside the cave was darkening. The silence that was Aaron's only reply stretched out and up and filled the cave.

Finally he said, "He could have killed you, Rechab. And that would have killed me."

"But he didn't," she said. "He didn't. I'm alive. I'll be more careful, I promise."

She could see something building up inside him—like steam in a lidded pot, ready to burst out. But at least he seemed to be listening for the moment—his rage buried if not completely subdued. "I think we should try to get out of here," she said again.

He lost it. He raised his voice, his face turning red, "I said we can't do that!"

Her eyes flooding with tears so that she couldn't see him clearly, Rechab turned away, using her bloodied hand to steady herself on the cave door. She paused on the threshold and glanced back at him.

"I need air. I'll make sure the guards go with me."

Aaron watched numbly as Rechab vanished into the night—gone into the darkness outside her little cave. The flicker of an oil lamp was all that illuminated this place where she lived, with its simple furnishings from Flora's caravan. Everything she had selected was small, elegant in a simple way, beautiful and fragile.

Like her.

He let out a groan and leaned on the cave wall, his forehead against his arm. His whole body shook.

Her bloodied hand.

Azeda's threats.

She might have been killed. Or taken into slavery. Or . . .

The ice that had knifed through his veins when Azeda threatened him was back, and far worse now.

And even worse still was Rechab herself hamstringing his response. He had not promised her that he wouldn't kill Azeda—the man was a hundred times a murderer, more than worthy of death!—but he couldn't go out and do the very thing she had begged him not to do, right on the heels of having chased her out of her own room with the heat of his anger.

Aaron cursed himself. He left the cave, venturing into the moonlight shining over the limestone ledge that looked over the village. Not far away were the entrances to the mines and his makeshift altar, where Rechab—his beautiful priestess, his bride—had led prayers every day.

And now she wanted to abandon the work. To run.

 RACHEL STARR THOMSON

Part of him wanted to say yes. To get her away to safety no matter what. But how could they leave this place when so many still needed them? When so many wrongs still needed to be made right? As fresh as though it had been yesterday, he remembered those who had not fought for his parents, for the people whose lives were destroyed along with theirs. He could not be so faithless, so fickle, here.

As lights began to flicker in the town, he caught sight of a small procession making their way up a side street. Worshipers of Kimash, he knew, going to offer oblations at the house of one of the Hill god's servants. The very idea of the Holy People prostrating themselves before the two-headed idol sickened him. Truly, they had come far from the glorious days of the past.

Kimash promised power—spells, incantations, favor. But the Great God had made them something more than themselves. He had made them different, better, more righteous than other nations.

A precious gift, and somewhere they had let it go. Much like Rechab would now let fear push her into giving up the Great God's work. He tasted gall as he pictured her leaving—running from him again.

As the worshippers disappeared in the shadows, an idea began to form in Aaron's mind.

He resisted it at first. But it did not go away, and as he thought on it, it seemed to him that shadows cleared and he knew just what to do.

He could strike a blow at Kimash and see Azeda taken down, all without lifting his own hand against him.

He would save the work and destroy the threat, and Rechab would never have to know.

———— ◆ ————

Flora remained blindfolded for a length of time she could not measure, until her whole body ached and she longed to sit down, to lie down, anything. The wound in her shoulder flared and throbbed, and she set her teeth against it. The only good thing about it was the distraction it served from the grief—from the butchery of her friends that was the last thing Amon had allowed her to see.

It all hurt more than the penance she'd done in the past, weighing her own arms down for prayer. Hurt more because she had no reason to think that all of this death and mistreatment was moving her or anyone else closer to the Great God in any way. It was all a waste—the pain, the lives, the grief.

And for that reason, Amon's rank treatment of her made her angry.

Something about being trapped in darkness and discomfort woke Flora's spirit. She could feel it awakening, like a phoenix from the ashy depression of her soul. It reminded her that she was, in fact, still alive; that her story was by no means over; and that as long as she still possessed strength and breath, she still possessed a reason to pray and a reason to protest.

Two words that, in sum, expressed the whole of her life from childhood until now.

So it was that when a servant, poking around the tent in what seemed to her an aimless succession of noises and small movements, suddenly whisked the blindfold off, she could feel her own eyes flashing back at him with righteous, indignant fury.

The servant seemed taken aback. A man of impossible-to-determine age, with wispy brown hair floating around a surprised bald spot, he blinked at her vacantly as though he hadn't realized there was a woman under there.

"Well, man?" she demanded. "What is it you want? You haven't come invading my quarters for nothing."

 RACHEL STARR THOMSON

At that the man seemed even more befuddled, more confused. He gaped at her.

She looked him up and down, assessing quickly that her first impression had been right and he was indeed a servant. A household slave, possibly not of the People—which would explain some of his dumbfounded nonresponse to her demands—unremarkable in every respect.

She switched to merchant pidgin. "Tell me what you want. Who sent you? Why?"

In a sudden fit of frustration, she strained against the ropes binding her to the tent pole. The momentary outburst sent a spasm of pain through her shoulder, and she let out an involuntary cry before gasping out, "Answer me! Stop gaping like a fish, man, and tell me what you want!"

At last the man, either cowed by Flora's tone or by her flailing attempt to free herself, took a few steps back. His face turned bright red.

And then he stuttered, "To . . . to see you."

The language was broken and heavily accented pidgin. Not from here, then—nor from anyplace anywhere near.

Her anger softened slightly. Who knew how this man had come to be a slave here, worlds away from his own home?

That glimmer of sympathy aside, his intrusion into her solitariness still angered her, as did his answer. Didn't he know better than to treat her like a curiosity? Hadn't he learned that friendship with her was dangerous?

"I'll thank you to leave me in peace," she said. "Your master did not send you here, nor would he be pleased to find you in this place."

Belatedly she added, "You can leave the blindfold off."

He seemed to be struggling to keep up. No hint that he intended to leave entered his face or his body language. But he did seem heartened by one word from her mouth, and he clung to it and repeated it.

"M-master."

"Yes," she said, impatience edging her voice.

But she didn't expect what he said next.

"Y-your master."

She frowned, leaning back so the ropes holding her went a little slack. Were they looser than before? Pain from her shoulder danced dark spots in her vision, and she closed her eyes for a moment.

He formed his words slowly, carefully. She thought it wasn't just the language tripping him up—his tongue didn't work as he wanted it to. His eyes were pale blue, strange and barbarian.

He pushed his words out with some effort. "Y-your master . . . is the Great . . . God."

Was it a question? A statement?

Confused, she nodded. Her anger had drained away, and her impatience with it. In the dim light of the tent, the man's eyes shone with urgency—with something he wanted badly to tell her.

But the words were not there.

He tried, stammering wordlessly twice more, licking his lips. Then he shook his head, seemingly frustrated, and hit his chest with his hand.

"M-my master. Too. Not . . . not . . . Amon."

"You are a worshiper of the Great God," Flora said softly.

He nodded. Tears came into his eyes. Slowly, he took a few steps closer to her. This time she let him come, quietly waiting to see what he would do.

He circled around behind her, and she felt the ropes loosen—not enough to release her entirely, but enough that she would be able to slide down and rest on the floor of the tent. The pressure came off her shoulder, bringing with it some relief.

He came back around, shaking his thinning head. She saw conflict in his pale eyes and knew he wanted to do more—knew he wanted to let her go entirely. To her surprise, though, it wasn't fear that wrestled with that desire—it was prudence. More than likely the tent was well guarded, and Flora could not possibly get far. Attempting to run would only bring greater trouble.

Obeying the ache in her legs, she slid down to the ground and let her arms move into a more relaxed position even as she leaned back against the pole.

"Thank you," she said.

He nodded, bobbing his head in a quick, nervous motion.

"I want to ask you so much," she said, looking up at him. "To know your story—why you're here. Why you did this for me. But I don't think you can tell me. Nor should you—we've all learned what danger attends befriending me."

A kind of confused benevolence in his eyes told her that indeed, he didn't understand. But he was pleased to see her resting, a little more at ease.

"Your compassion has lifted my heart," she told him, hoping he would at least understand her tone.

It made her want to weep with grief and gratitude to know that she still had a friend in Amon's camp.

After everything that had happened, it seemed like another sign that she was not forgotten.

CHAPTER 17

Aaron's hands shook as he regarded the bloody knife in his hands and told himself he had done justly.

Outside the cave in the side of the mountain, voices clamored for answers. For him. It seemed the whole village had gathered to demand an audience.

The night before was a dark blot on his memory, a shadowy dream he was loath to admit had been real. The bitterness of Azeda's triumphant threats still twisted his mouth, and the fear he'd felt at the danger to Rechab. Scenes from earlier days played across his memory too: the people's refusal to come to the hearing; Azeda's smug, mocking expression. The knowledge that he had signed away Flora's gold, a significant and secret part of her business, and that it would make no difference except to enslave her interests to a man who did not deserve to live.

A man very like the one who had destroyed Aaron's family, so many years ago.

Blood had dried along the knife blade. Dried black. The spots where metal shone through flickered in the light from outside.

Anger had ruled him last night. Had driven him. Rechab's calming, beautiful presence had assuaged it for a moment, but she had run from him in the end—left him to his passions. To his memories. To his desire to make things *right*.

So he had gone out into the night and found the woman.

A witch. He knew that. He knew that when he went to her.

A shrine to Kimash glowed in the chamber in her house. He did not look at it. He turned up his nose and stared down at her instead.

"Can you do what I ask?" he had said.

She peered back up at him, counting the money he had dropped onto the table before her with her hands.

"For good coinage I can do anything," she rasped.

"But it must not be just for that. The man deserves to die."

She cackled. "Oh yes. He does."

"Has he wronged you?"

"Azeda has wronged everyone. He deserves death a hundred times over."

He should have asked why no one had killed him then. Why this woman had not used her power to kill him. Instead he felt like a man of courage, a man who alone would do what was necessary or hire it done.

For the sake of the people. And for Rechab.

She closed her eyes and began to drone. The air grew darker—and darker till it seemed the lights had been snuffed out, and the only light came from the shrine—but even that was not light. It was an emptiness. An emptiness that lived. Too late he realized she was invoking, incanting.

Then her eyes shot open. Her pupils were gone; her eyes were yellow and fixed on him. She gasped. "The girl!" she said. "The girl is not Flora. Kimash wants—"

 RACHEL STARR THOMSON

That was when he had killed her.

He clutched the knife handle until his knuckles ached. Outside, the clamor was growing. They wanted him. And Rechab.

He had to stop hiding here, stop staring at his guilt in the form of a blood-encrusted handle, and go help her.

She found him before he had a chance to force himself to her side. Her shadow blocked the light from outside. Her face was tear-streaked.

"Aaron. They say Azeda is dead too."

"What?" His heart beat faster. He had not thought the witch had finished her spell.

"They say he dropped dead in the night. They blame us. Aaron, what did you do?"

"I didn't kill him."

"But the woman—"

"She was a priestess of Kimash. A servant of the very evil that threatens to enslave this land."

Rechab sighed, voice heavy with crying and with a weary, helpless fear. "And her followers are legion in this village. They do not want the Great God here, Aaron. It's no wonder they didn't come to the judgment when we called it. It doesn't matter what we do; they do not want us."

His throat threatened to close. He had not meant to do this to her. He had wanted to protect her, to make something of her—to help her become what the Great God wanted.

"Aaron—" Her voice choked out as she struggled not to cry. He jumped to his feet, dropping the knife. He wanted to rush to her side, to comfort her. He stopped himself and stood, quivering.

"Rechab, tell me what I can do."

"They've gathered to curse us and demand answers. The elders are outside. They want money—restitution. Just give it to them, Aaron. Give it to them and tell them we'll leave. We shouldn't have come here."

Crushing disappointment weighed his head down. He had not thought she would give up so quickly.

"Azeda is dead," she said, getting control of her voice again, "so maybe things will get better here. Just give the elders control of the mines. Let them finish the reforms. Surely they will. They represent the village. Maybe they'll do what's right. We just need to leave."

"Yes," he said woodenly. "I'll tell them."

The darkness in the witch's hut the night before seemed to hang around his head. Mocking him. Declaring in all the voices clangoring outside that it had won, because he was too much of a coward to see things through.

Because he had come to care too deeply for this girl, this gift who stood before him and begged him to make everything go away.

He went to exit the cave, expecting her to move out of his way, but she stayed where she was so that he was forced to brush past her. He paused, and they stood together for a moment, silent, heavy with silence, and he promised her without words that he would make things better.

She seemed to understand.

The sun struck him nearly blind, but he strode on, toward the noise. Flora's retinue—better armed and organized than the villagers by far—held back a mob. It seemed most of the village had come out, belligerent and demanding some kind of payment for the wrongs done them. The elders, all six of them, stood at the fore.

Aaron approached the oldest and noisiest of them all. The man accosted him before he could open his mouth.

 Rachel Starr Thomson

"And there's the mouthpiece!" he said. "What does your mistress say, boy? Will she answer for her crimes?"

"She has done nothing," Aaron said, narrowing his eyes.

"Nothing! She has killed the priestess of Kimash! She has killed our exalted head of . . ."

"How dare you?" Aaron shouted the words. They fell over the crowd and stilled it. His anger, rising and reddening his face, boiled over.

"How dare you flaunt your idolatry and your injustice? Who are the dead? A witch and a tyrant! Oppressors who kept your people in slavery and sin! And you dare accuse my mistress of a crime? If justice held any sway in this place, you all would die!"

He climbed a small rocky outcrop so the whole mob could see him, ignoring the elders.

"Some of your own came to us when we approached this village. Complaining of wrongs left unrighted, children enslaved, lives lost."

His eyes swept the crowd. The three beggars were there—hanging back at the fringes, like they always did. He wondered how they felt about all that had happened. If they rued the day they had begged Flora's help.

But he could not bear to leave their pleas unanswered.

"These men have enslaved you!" he shouted. "They have corrupted you. How dare you take their part now? Flora would free you! She would offer you help!"

His eyes swept over the crowd and rested on the plumes of smoke rising from the smelting fires at the base of the mines.

Copper and tin and bronze; great wealth. Wealth this rabble would only abuse. The reforms in the mines would not be finished; more people would die and be crippled and turn into idol worshippers, all for the sake of greed.

He knew what Rechab wanted him to do.

But he could not do it. The words twisted on his tongue and soured in his gut. Standing here, commanding their craven attention, other words came to him. Inspired words.

"No, we will not leave you to your own already failed devices," he shouted. "People of Nachush, your oppressor is dead. The witch of Kimash is dead. From this moment on, this village belongs to the Great God, and it will serve him. In the name of Flora Laurentii, I declare this place to be under the Great God's control. His laws will be enforced. And you will be free."

He raised his fist. "I swear," he repeated. "You will be free."

———◆◆———

At sea on the dark waves, Alack was thinking of Rechab.

He wondered where she was—if she was still in Shalem with her father, or if they had returned to Bethabara for the rest of the season. He hoped she was safe, and that whatever marriage arrangements Nadab the Trader was in the midst of making were neither finalized nor yet acted upon. Everything in him ached at the knowledge that Rechab would soon be another man's. He only hoped that Nadab would take his last act of begging before he left Bethabara seriously and would choose to give her to someone outside of Shalem—someone she could feel safe with.

On a Westland ship riding over waves under the faint beginnings of stars, Alack pondered how far he had come. And he wondered if he was not here, after all, because he'd wanted to seek the Great God, or save his people, or become a prophet. He wondered if he was here because of Rechab—because he'd accepted at last that it was hopeless

     RACHEL STARR THOMSON

to desire her and had not been brave enough to stay and watch her marry someone else.

Maybe, after all, he was just a coward running away in the most effective way he could think of.

He didn't really know. His own heart, he thought, was as fathomless as the sea—and who knew what mysteries, what lights and what shadows, lay in its deepest places?

He had not been able to escape his love for Rechab, if indeed that was why he had chosen to join Kol Abaddon in the desert. His vision of the wadi and the lamb, repeated with Rechab and a dragon, still haunted him. And when he looked up at the night sky and the constellations telling stories overhead, it was Rechab he saw in the figure of Isha—the beloved—racing toward her doom in the waiting maw of the dragon.

He stared up now, watching for the stars to come out as the sky began to darken. He wished Kol Abaddon were here to talk to him about them, if there was anything more to be said.

He smiled a little—sadly—at the remembrance of what Kol Abaddon had told him. "Ask the Great God yourself." Alack had asked the Great God many things by now. Most of his questions went unanswered—and when he got visions, which he could only believe came from the Invisible One of the Holy People himself—they led him places he did not want to go.

They had led him to this ship, where he was an emissary for his enemies against his own people.

He had been turning a stiff piece of bread in his hand for the last hour. It was too stale, with a hard raft of mold up one side, to eat. Finally he cocked his arm back and threw it hard, out to sea.

"Cast your bread upon the waters," he murmured, repeating an old proverb Naam had recited when he was a boy. "For after many days you may find it again."

Naam. His father. One more person to miss.

Alack was not one to feel sorry for himself. But out here, without even his moldy piece of bread to lend familiar company, the loneliness that washed over him threated to crush his very soul.

The loneliness was much worse than what he'd known on the journey to the Westland. Locked in the hold with the slaves, he'd been playing the loyal companion. Kol Abaddon had been by his side, and the Great God, presumably, had been out there in front of them somewhere—directing their journey.

Kol Abaddon would say the Great God was still directing it. But Alack didn't know how to reconcile that with where he found himself now.

No more the loyal companion, he was a traitor now—a traitor to his own people. No more the voice of the Great God, but the messenger of Sabrus Caelius.

To add to his misery, ships were not much easier to ride as a statesman than they were as a slave. The sea still bucked and rolled; the ship still rode waves higher than hills; and Alack still turned green as seaweed and clung to the deck rails in abject unhappiness and fear.

The Westlanders aboard mostly ignored him. A few servants had been assigned to see to his comfort, and they did their best. A few soldiers pointedly kept their eyes on him—like there was anywhere he could go. But for the most part, they all left him to himself.

Wrapped in a deep red Westlander cloak, Alack stood at the rail as the world around him pitched, staring out over black waters tipped with dull white. The last traces of sunset still lingered in the sky, ushering in deep darkness. The air, wet with spray, made his cloak and his head heavy.

His eyes stung.

 RACHEL STARR THOMSON

A savior, are you? his inner voice taunted. *A prophet. On your way to help your people.*

"O Great God," he mouthed, the words becoming vocal to his surprise as he said them. "I don't know what I am doing. I don't know where you are."

His voice took on some strength. There were others on deck, but they couldn't hear him over the ever-present noise of the sea. And he wanted to shout the words—to spit them into the darkening night.

"You must be a trickster!" he complained. "As bad as Kimash, or the gods of the Westland! Why else bring me here? Why else let this happen?"

Bitterness twisted his voice and tasted like gall on his lips. His voice took on urgency. *"How could you let this happen?"*

In answer, Alack saw a vision.

He did not know at first what it was—he thought it was reality. A massive, serpentine head rose from the black waves before his eyes, climbing higher on a long, sinuous neck; rising higher than the deck, and the rail, and the mast, until it towered above the boat. Its eyes burned like fire. Its scales were black—no, Alack thought, *blackened,* like something seared in flame. Wings—six wings—unfolded from the length of its legless, armless body.

Leviathan; the Dragon; the Worm.

It brought its great head and its dreadful length crashing down on the boat, cleaving it in half in a soundless splintering of wood and rope and tar, and then Alack was in the water, and sinking—sinking into the deep.

Toward an orange, hazy light.

Far below the water, something burned.

He sank peacefully. He felt no fear—no panic. Only a deeper, more terrible dread.

He sank for years. For centuries.

Millennia passed.

The light shone from a far distant past.

At last he drew near. Beneath the water he could make out spires and rooftops; temples and palaces; houses and markets. He could make out the porticos of pools and the lines of streets. A city—vast, vaster and grander than the Holy City, greater and richer than Avia, broader and more civilized than imagination.

The light came from its lamps and its altars, still burning here beneath the water.

He wondered how it was that such a place had been forgotten—that no one in the Sacred Land knew of it. And then his eyes were opened still further, and he saw that the world under the water stretched out over a great landscape, the size of the whole world, with still other cities, and temples, and towers.

His foot touched the tip of a tower.

Thousands of feet high, it stretched leagues above the city itself. As Alack came to settle on its stone, he realized it had never been finished.

It seemed as though someone had tried to build it to reach the surface of the water.

No indeed, a voice said in his heart, *but to reach the heavens in the world before the flood.*

And then, from beneath the glow of the lamps came a growing darkness—a shadow that gathered as gloom in the streets and took on palpable force as it grew, spreading, solidifying, and radiating upward and then sweeping up with sudden speed, swallowing the tower where Alack stood until it was just beneath his feet and the dread he had felt boiled into instant and terrible fear.

     Rachel Starr Thomson

He came back to himself scrambling on his back on the deck, feet desperately trying to find purchase on the always-slick boards. Someone was grabbing at his arm, which he realized only after he had already struck out at the man.

Thankfully, the soldier took no offense. He hauled Alack roughly to his feet and stared intently at him.

"Are you all right?" he asked.

"Yes, I . . . I'm fine. I'm all right." Alack pulled his arm out of the man's grasp and tried to straighten out his tunic and gather his cloak back around him in a vain attempt to recover his dignity. The truth was he wasn't even fully sure where he was—not back in possession of his faculties enough to know truth from vision.

Ah, but visions are truth, said the voice inside.

"It seems you took a tumble," the soldier said, still staring hard at Alack.

"I slipped," he said. "The sea is . . . rough."

The soldier chuckled a little at that, and Alack heard sympathy in the tone. "On you especially, it would seem. I wish you a smoother voyage, boy, before we reach land. Some get their sea legs after a few days."

"It has been a week already," Alack said weakly, still trying to pull his thoughts back enough to focus on the present reality. "I do not think my body knows any legs but the kind that walk on land."

The soldier slapped him on the shoulder. "Well, then, may the voyage go quickly."

Alack nodded, and the soldier moved away. In his place, all the images of the vision crowded back—the sea serpent, the fiery glow, the city beneath the waves. The world that once was, swallowed in a deluge.

And the soldier's words sank in.

He did not want the voyage to go quickly. When it was over, they would come to the desert wastes of the Sacred Land, and to its villages, and its mountain and its beautiful, golden city.

Alack would face his own king, his own people, as the mouthpiece of destruction from the West.

That moment, he dreaded above all else.

⸺ ◆ ⸺

That very day, a rebellion had begun in the heart of the Sacred Land. The elders in the village of Nachush, with a few of the most ardent of Kimash's devotees, attempted to drive off the newcomers who had taken over their mines and their authority, but Aaron led Flora's armed retinue in putting them down. The fight was swift and decisive.

Only hours later, Rechab—trembling, trapped, and guilt-stricken—led the people of the village in a vow to the Great God, who alone would be worshiped on that ground from that day forth.

That finished, Aaron and five of his fellow servants oversaw court where the elders were at last held responsible for their crimes against the people. Confident now that the balance of power had fully shifted, the aggrieved came forth. Payments were made. Children freed. And the most guilty executed for the blood they had shed.

It was a day of righteous judgment, the first in that valley for generations. Rechab saw it and acknowledged the justice of every decision Aaron made. She told herself that this was the will of the Great God. She tried to maintain her peace and her leadership in Flora's place—for Flora's sake, for the Great God.

Less than two weeks later, the first of the migrants began to come. Word had carried that the Great God's law held sway in one faithful

 RACHEL STARR THOMSON

valley. Some of the newcomers were workers, farmers, miners weary with injustice and seeking a better life.

Many were young men, zealous, inspired, and armed.

And Rechab feared what would happen next.

EPILOGUE

In a jail cell beneath a grand palace in Avia, the coastal capital of the Westland, Kol Abaddon sat and stank in the darkness.

The prophet of the Sacred Land had hardly stirred for weeks. Not since the boy came to say good-bye. Kol Abaddon had promised him then that he would join him, and he intended to—as soon as the Great God let him out.

But that, he knew, would not be until he bent.

The cell was hardly big enough for a man. It was one in a long row, all barred by iron grates and patrolled by a lone guard with a key that jangled on a ring. The row of cells was eerily silent, as it had been for days, because Kol Abaddon was the only prisoner. All others had been released or executed in the games to celebrate the ascendance of the new emperor.

The Sword of Heaven, Kol Abaddon mused. Sabrus Caelius. The fulfillment of so many of his dreams.

The prophet closed his eyes in the darkness, as though he could shut out the memories that way. It was just as dark in the cell as it was behind his eyes, but with his lids drawn tight he could try to stop thought, stop any presence beyond his own from intruding on his internal world.

The prophet let out a long, shaky sigh, and he stretched his legs out before him.

He would not bend.

He had not come this far to give in.

The boy had nearly wrecked things. With his insistence on helping the slaves—who just sold themselves right back into slavery anyway, as Kol Abaddon could have predicted they would, and that without any help from the gift of prophecy—with his visions of lambs and saving help. He might still ruin it. Better that Kol Abaddon sit in this cell and rot, far away, where he would only hear in rumors if at all what had become of the people who killed his family.

Long, long ago, the Holy People had ceased to be anything but that to him.

The memories tormented him now as they had for decades.

People thought it was the Great God's visions that tormented him in the wilderness. People thought he howled for the pain and suffering of what he saw. But no—no, those visions of the marching army, of terrible devastation unleashed on the People were his comfort. They were his reward. They were the answer to the real reason he writhed and howled in the desert night—the reason of his pain, his loss, his grief, the injustice that had never been answered.

The People would be swept away on the bloody tide of the Sword of Heaven, come from the sea on the swell of the dragon. Kol Abaddon, if he had his way, would die with them, free at last from all his troubles. He would die happy, knowing that his grievance had been addressed in the end. For twenty years he had gone to them—in the courts of Shalem until he was thrown out of the city for good, and then in the smaller towns like Bethabara, and the villages, and he had given them the message of judgment and watched them turn stony hearts even harder. His message was judgment in itself. When the sword came, not

　　RACHEL STARR THOMSON

one would be able to say they had not known. The Great God was angry with them, and they carried their own guilt on their heads.

The pain inside him was beginning to gnaw. He shifted, his feet twitching, his legs starting to cord as his muscles cramped. He let out a low sound, a hum, a protest.

Things had grown unexpectedly complicated in the last few weeks.

For one thing, he cared about the boy.

He hadn't meant to. He had meant to keep the lad fully at arm's length. But it hadn't worked, and now he was worried about him—sailing across the sea, going home in the position of prophet to the court, without a lick of experience and even less sense.

But there was something else.

Something else that made him—not *consider,* but think of, allow into his consciousness in barely viable snatches—the thought that he could bend after all.

There was Flora Laurentii.

Like Kol Abaddon, Flora was a legend all over the Sacred Land. A symbol. An archetype, and barely aware of it. But if Kol Abaddon symbolized the Great God's anger, Flora symbolized something far more frightening to the desert madman.

Flora symbolized hunger and devotion. She was everything the Holy People were supposed to be and were not.

She was the reason the Great God wanted him to bend.

People called Kol Abaddon mad. The "mad prophet," the insane voice in the wilderness. They were right. He was. Half-mad, anyway. But not because of the Great God's visions. Kol Abaddon was half-mad because of his grief and his bitterness and his insatiable hunger for revenge, *and because what the Great God most wanted him to do, he refused to do—and he had been refusing for over twenty years.*

Comes the Dragon 241

He let loose a cry. The fit took him, and he writhed on the filthy floor of the cell and hit his head against the wall until he bled. Footsteps pounded the length of the hall outside and then stopped as the guard stared, but Kol Abaddon hardly knew he was there, and did not care.

When the fit ended he lay panting, staring up at the ceiling of the cell, and the ceiling lifted as he stared.

In its place was light.

A light that waited, expectant, for him to do what he was meant to do.

"No," he said, licking the froth away from his lips. "No. It is not right. I can't. I can't."

The light said nothing. Only waited.

Tears came into his eyes and began to run down his face. He felt small. He became aware of pain—his head throbbing, bruises on his legs and arms from the thrashing. His back ached. He was hungry . . . hungry down in the pit of his stomach.

"I am Kol Abaddon," he whispered. The Voice of Destruction.

And then there was Flora again—in memory this time.

"What is your name?" she had asked him.

"I do not have one," he had answered.

"I have learned that in the service of the Great God, one finds one's name, one does not lose it," she had told him.

He had not been able to get those words out of his head.

And now he also remembered that she had said he was a man, a human being, with needs, and that she wanted to meet them if she possibly could. Right now he wanted to ask her to pay his way out of this cell, to give him a meal, and maybe a new robe, and maybe— maybe—water to wash or even bathe in.

Does this mean, a voice in his thoughts said, that you are bending?

But justice, he said.

Can you not leave that to me?

But you will *forgive.*

Is that not my prerogative?

No. For I have a claim. They killed my family.

And I have many claims. Even on you. Yet you dismiss them—run from them. For twenty years now.

And then the voice called him by his name.

Kol Abaddon *heard* it—as clearly as if the guard, who had wandered away when the fit ended, had spoken it. He could not describe the voice, but he heard it audibly in the air and he trembled because of it, like a child who has run away and hears his father calling him—and who is both angry that he has been found and will be made to return home and also very, very glad.

Will you do it? the voice asked.

Kol Abaddon shook his shaggy head, and tears ran down his sun-blistered face. "I am too old," he said out loud. "I have been running too long."

You still know where it is, Kohan. You have never forgotten.

"They won't listen. They never do. They turn their hearts to stone."

And yet Alack is real. He listened. Flora Laurentii is real. She has given her life to listen. Will you leave them with nothing to hear?

You can show them yourself where it is, he stubbornly replied.

But I have chosen you to do it.

There was silence in the cell as Kol Abaddon stretched out his aching legs and stared sullenly into the shadows.

Do you remember the stars? the voice asked.

"Yes," he said; "someday I even hope to see them again."

What is *in* the stars, Prophet?

He folded his arms and replied, aloud, "The Dragon."

And?

"And Isha, the Beloved."

Isha, who represented the Holy People, running into the waiting mouth of the Dragon. Confirmation of Kol Abaddon's terrible message, written across the sky.

Whose Beloved is she?" the voice asked.

Kol Abaddon refused to answer.

WHOSE?

In the darkness below the palace, Kol Abbadon trembled.

"Yours," he whispered.

Overhead, the ground shook with the tramping feet of warriors—hundreds upon hundreds of soldiers, the mercenary armies of Sabrus Caelius amassing for invasion and conquest.

Before his eyes, Kol Abaddon's cell door creaked open. The guard was nowhere in sight. Just beyond clear vision, he saw something like a shaft of light move through the hall, and then it was gone.

The door stood wide open, waiting for him.

Slowly, he pushed himself to his feet and stood unbalanced for a moment. Holding on to the wall for support. With his head bent so he would not smack it on the low ceiling, the prophet of the Sacred Land left his prison.

It was time to go home.

Bent at last.

The story concludes in *Beloved,*
Book 3 of The Prophet Trilogy

Rachel would love to hear from you!

You can visit her and interact online:
Web: **www.rachelstarrthomson.com**
Facebook: **www.facebook.com/RachelStarrThomsonWriter**
Twitter: **@writerstarr**

THE SEVENTH WORLD TRILOGY

Worlds Unseen   Burning Light   Coming Day

For five hundred years the Seventh World has been ruled by a tyrannical empire—and the mysterious Order of the Spider that hides in its shadow. History and truth are deliberately buried, the beauty and treachery of the past remembered only by wandering Gypsies, persecuted scholars, and a few unusual seekers. But the past matters, as Maggie Sheffield soon finds out. It matters because its forces will soon return and claim lordship over her world, for good or evil.

The Seventh World Trilogy is an epic fantasy, beautiful, terrifying, pointing to the realities just beyond the world we see.

"An excellent read, solidly recommended for fantasy readers."

– Midwest Book Review

"A wonderfully realistic fantasy world. Recommended."

– Jill Williamson, Christy-Award-Winning Author
of *By Darkness Hid*

"Epic, beautiful, well-written fantasy that sings of Christian truth."

– Rael, reader

Available everywhere online or special order from your local bookstore.

THE ONENESS CYCLE

Exile   Hive   Attack   Renegade   Rise

The supernatural entity called the Oneness holds the world together. What happens if it falls apart?

In a world where the Oneness exists, nothing looks the same. Dead men walk. Demons prowl the air. Old friends peel back their mundane masks and prove as supernatural as angels. But after centuries of battling demons and the corrupting powers of the world, the Oneness is under a new threat—its greatest threat. Because this time, the threat comes from within.

Fast-paced contemporary fantasy.

"Plot twists and lots of edge-of-your-seat action, I had a hard time putting it down!"
—Alexis

"Finally! The kind of fiction I've been waiting for my whole life!"
—Mercy Hope, FaithTalks.com

"I sped through this short, fast-paced novel, pleased by the well-drawn characters and the surprising plot. Thomson has done a great job of portraying difficult emotional journeys . . . Read it!"
—Phyllis Wheeler, The Christian Fantasy Review

Available everywhere online or special order from your local bookstore.

TAERITH

When he rescues a young woman named Lilia from bandits, Taerith Romany is caught in a web of loyalties: Lilia is the future queen of a spoiled king, and though Taerith is not allowed to love her, neither he can bring himself to leave her without a friend. Their lives soon intertwine with the fiercely proud slave girl, Mirian, whose tragic past and wild beauty make her the target of the king's unscrupulous brother.

The king's rule is only a knife's edge from slipping—and when it does, all three will be put to the ultimate test. In a land of fog and fens, unicorns and wild men, Taerith stands at the crossroads of good and evil, where men are vanquished by their own obsessions or saved by faith in higher things.

"Devastatingly beautiful . . . I am amazed at every chapter how deeply you've caused us to care for these characters."
—Gabi

"Deeply satisfying." —Kapezia

"Rachel Starr Thomson is an artist, and every chapter of Taerith is like a painting . . . beautiful."
—Brittany Simmons

Available everywhere online or special order from your local bookstore.

ANGEL IN THE WOODS

Hawk is a would-be hero in search of a giant to kill or a maiden to save. The trouble is, when he finds them, there are forty-some maidens—and they call their giant "the Angel." Before he knows what's happening, Hawk is swept into the heart of a patchwork family and all of its mysteries, carried away by their camaraderie—and falling quickly in love.

But the outside world cannot be kept at bay forever. Suspecting the Giant of hiding a treasure, the wealthy and influential Widow Brawnlyn sets out to tear the family apart and bring the Giant to destruction any way she can. And her two principle weapons are Hawk—and the truth.

Caught between the terrible truths he discovers about the family's past and the unalterable fact that he has come to love them, Hawk must face his fears and overcome his flaws if he is to rescue the Angel in the woods.

"A beautiful tale of finding oneself, honor and heroism; a story I will not soon forget."
— Szoch

"The more I think about it, the more truth and beauty I find in the story."
—H. A. Titus

Available everywhere online or special order from your local bookstore.

REAP THE WHIRLWIND

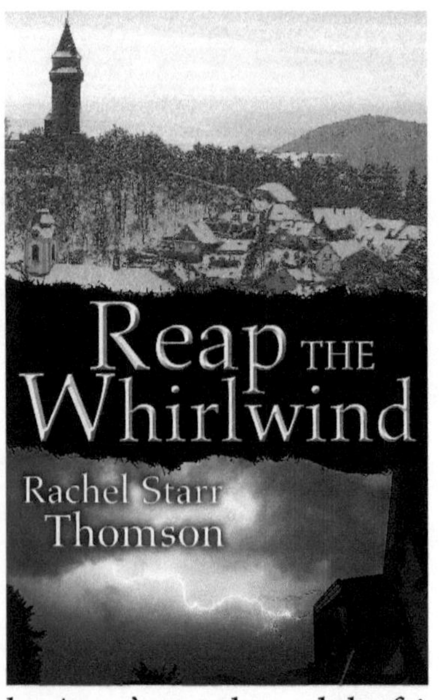

Beren is a city in constant unrest: ruled by a ruthless upper class and harried by a band of rebels who want change. Its one certainty is that the two sides do not, and will not, meet.

But children know little of sides or politics, and Anna and Kyara—a princess and a peasant girl—let their chance meeting grow into a deep friendship. Until the day Kyara's family is slaughtered by Anna's people, and the friendship comes to an abrupt end.

Years later, Kyara is a rebel—bitter, hard, and violent. Anna's efforts to fight the political system she belongs to avail little. Neither is a child anymore—but neither has ever forgotten the power of their long-ago friendship. When a secret plot brings the rebellion to a fiery head, both young women know it is too late to save the land they love.

But is it too late to save each other?

Available everywhere online.

LADY MOON

When Celine meets Tomas, they are in a cavern on the moon where she has been languishing for thirty days after being banished by her evil uncle for throwing a scrub brush at his head. Tomas is a charming and eccentric Immortal, hanging out on the moon because he's procrastinating his destiny—meeting, and defeating, Celine's uncle.

A pair of magic rings send them back to earth, where Celine insists on returning home and is promptly thrown into the dungeon. Her uncle, Ignus Umbria, is up to no good, and his latest caper threatens to devour the whole countryside. He doesn't want Celine getting in the way. More than that, he wants to force Tomas into a confrontation—and Tomas, who has fallen in love with Celine, cannot procrastinate any longer.

Lady Moon is a fast-paced, humorous adventure in a world populated by mad magicians, walking rosebushes, thieving scullery maids, and other improbable things. And of course, the most improbable—and magical—thing of all: true love.

"Celine's sarcastic 'languishing' immediately put me in mind of Patricia C. Wrede's Dealing with Dragons series—a fairy tale that gently makes fun of the usual fairy tale tropes. And once again, Rachel Starr Thomson doesn't disappoint."

— H. A. Titus

"Funny and quirky fantasy."

Available everywhere online.

THE PROPHET TRILOGY

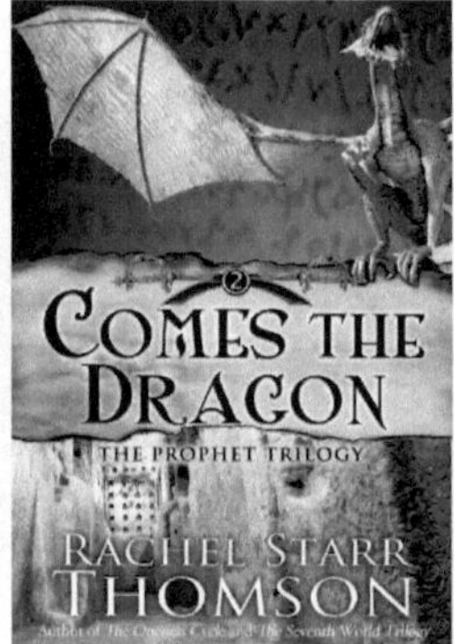

Abaddon's Eve   Comes the Dragon   Beloved

A prophet and his apprentice.
A runaway and a wealthy widow marked as an outcast.

They alone can see the terrible judgment
marching on their land.

But can they do anything to stop it?

The Prophet Trilogy is a fantasy set in
a near-historical world of deserts, temples,
and spiritual forces that vie
for the hearts of men.

Available everywhere online or special order from your local bookstore.

Short Fiction by Rachel Starr Thomson

Butterflies Dancing

Fallen Star

Of Men and Bones

Ogres Is

Journey

Magdalene

The City Came Creeping

Wayfarer's Dream

War With the Muse

Shields of the Earth

And more!

Available as downloads for Kindle, Kobo, Nook, iPad, and more!

www.ingramcontent.com/pod-product-compliance
Lightning Source LLC
Chambersburg PA
CBHW051302210726
48287CB00002B/634